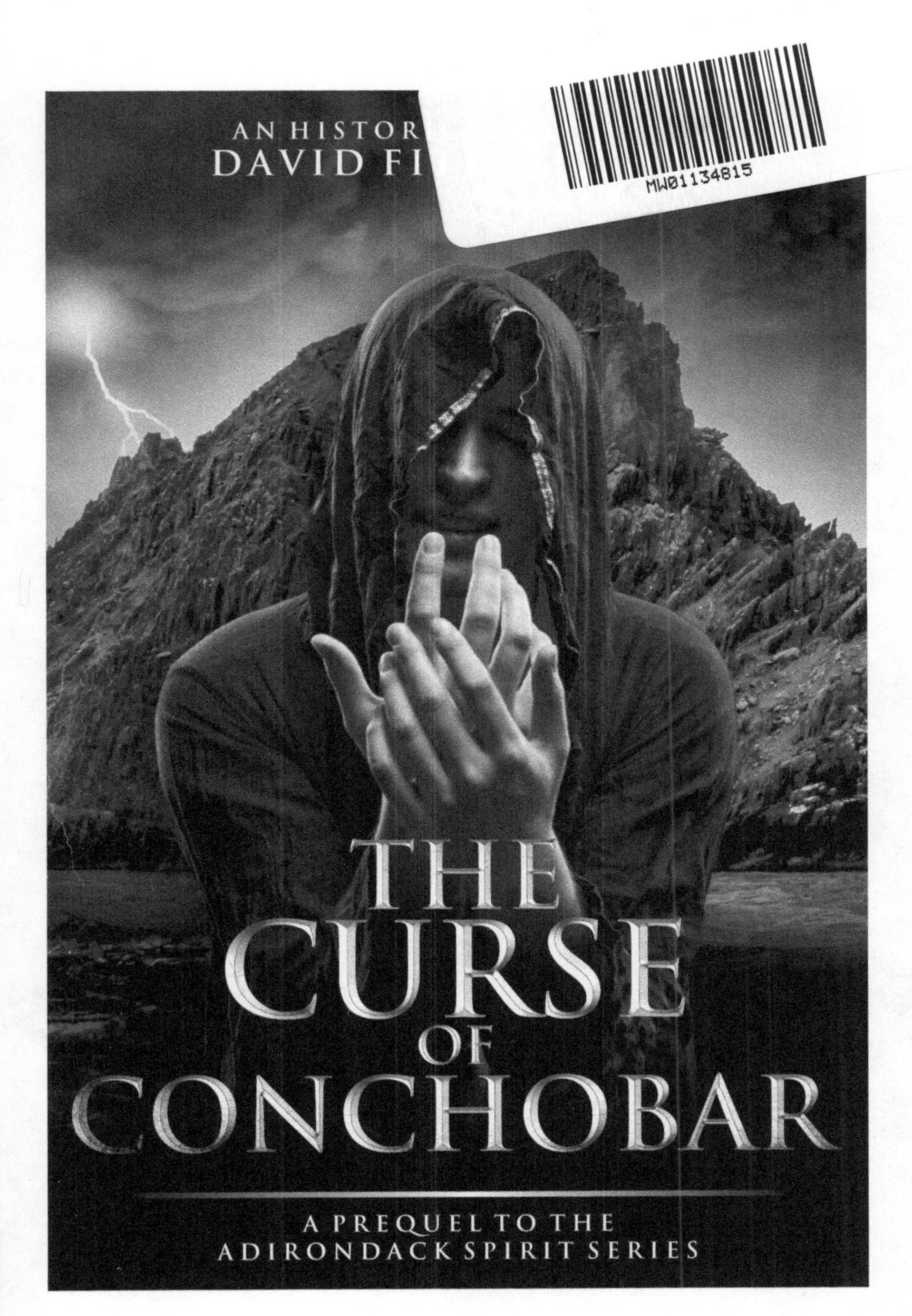

outskirts press

David Fitz-Gerald

The Curse of Conchobar—A Prequel to the Adirondack Spirit Series

v2.0

Outskirts Press, Inc.
http://www.outskirtspress.com

ISBN: 978-1-9772-3815-3

Library of Congress Control Number: 2021900068

Cover design by: @padrondesign

PRINTED IN THE UNITED STATES OF AMERICA

Dedicated to the memory of my mother,
Carolyn Ann Schultz,
whose wish finally came true.

Chapter 1

Spring AD 549

I hear a voice. Could it be God? Am I dead? I try to open my eyes. It should be easy, yet my eyes will not open. What is the voice saying? It seems nearby and far away at the same time. I don't understand the language. It dawns on me that there are several voices.

I try to recall where I am. I remember dragging my boat ashore and falling to the ground. How long ago did it happen? I should get up. I wonder if the voices mean danger or assistance. My body seems unwilling to move—not so much as a finger or toe obeys my command. Perhaps I should be glad that I am not in pain, yet feeling *nothing* is terrifying.

Something touches my mouth. My lips separate and I realize that someone's fingers are holding my mouth open. A trickle of water moistens my lips, crosses my teeth, and wets my tongue. It tastes like mana, better than I imagine the nectar consumed by God would taste. I feel a hand beneath my head, lifting me slightly. A little more water causes me to swallow. My head is gently set back on the ground. I try to wiggle my toes.

Water splashes on my face. I gasp for air. The shock of cold, salty water on my skin brings back the pain, and I instinctively curl into a ball.

I feel a pair of hands at my back, beneath my shoulder blades. I'm swiftly lifted in the air. Someone must expect me to stand, but my legs fail to find support beneath me and I crumble to the ground once more.

I am lifted and tossed into the water. The voices are louder. I feel the hands of several people dunking me swiftly, then I'm back on the ground again. Sensation has returned to my body.

My lips are parted once more. Something has been placed between my cheek and gums. My mouth waters and I sense the faint taste of meat.

I feel fingers on my face. Slippery hands rub something slimy on my skin. It still feels dry. I picture a mud puddle at the end of a dry day. I recall being in the sun for days, weeks, perhaps a month or more. Then I remember being lost at sea. An accidental voyage that began with a sudden storm.

Greasy fingers pry my eyes open and I see the face of a stranger. Intense brown eyes are surrounded by shiny blue skin. The man releases his hold on my face and my eyes remain open. I blink rapidly, aware of a dozen men and half as many canoes on the flat bank of a wide river.

A couple of the men hoist my body into the air with as much care as they would provide a fallen deer that they planned to butcher. They drop me into the center of one of their slender canoes. One takes the front and the other gets into the back. My little fishing boat is tied with a short rope to the back of their canoe. The men paddle steadily, keeping pace with the canoes ahead of them.

The nourishment provided by the dried meat and water have my senses functioning again. I'm now aware of how weak my body is. I'm barely strong enough to hold up my head or move to a sitting position. Instead I lie here quietly staring into the sky as the canoe moves steadily against the river current. I spend the day trying to recall how I came to be in this predicament and trying to figure out where I am.

I don't know how long I was on the riverbank. I don't remember reaching the shore or seeing land from the expanse of open ocean. I recall day after endless day of floating wherever the current cared to take me. It could have been weeks. It could have been months.

I try to distract myself from worrying about whether the men who paddle the canoe have rescued or captured me. I am glad that I can recall my homeland, but I keep returning to thoughts about one fateful morning and the events that brought me here. That morning, I took a few hours off from chiseling steps on the cliffs of my island mountain. I wished to try my hand at some fishing. A storm gathered, so abruptly that I was unable to paddle back to shore. The harsh wind blew so forcefully, it was all I could do to keep my boat afloat. I quickly lost my oars and was left with the lunch I had packed in a pail and my fishing gear.

As a result of my fateful fishing trip, I spent countless weeks floating in despair, tossed around by the whims of wind and waves. I despise my memories of those endless days and nights while lost at sea, yet my mind keeps returning to those bleak and perilous times.

Oh, how I long for the majestic island of emerald and stone. I regret having dodged Lector Beccán, taking his long green robe and the small boat. In my seventeen years, I had been permitted to go fishing only once. The ocean seemed full of promise and adventure, but everything changed after being lost at sea. I no longer feel drawn to the ocean; I despise it. Perhaps riding in a canoe is better. It helps to know there is land on either side of the river.

My head feels so fuzzy, I can hardly think, but concern pushes through. I know that my survival is a miracle, but I have plenty of concern about my current situation. The men who rescued me from drought and starvation look like demons and carry all manners of weaponry. It's just the sort of scene that Lector Beccán's readings described. I can picture the Abbot, the Prior, and the Sub-Prior nodding behind my proctor as he reads. I wish I had the strength and energy to sit up in the canoe.

After paddling all day, the men stop an hour before sunset. They argue and fight well into the evening before it gets quiet. I lay among ferns outside of the light of the fire, forgotten until morning.

Just after sunrise, two men approach me. I cower and try to retreat among the ferns. I wilt under the scrutiny of intense eyes that gaze through holes in a mask made from a cat-like creature that looks evil. I look away quickly, yet I can't shake the image. I'm sure the mask is meant to seem menacing. The cat must have died while snarling, and the imposing incisor teeth look like they could rip a person apart in a single bite. Black hair points from the top of its triangular ears, and a white beard makes the cat seem twice as large as it otherwise would be. I imagine myself disemboweled by long sharp claws as the squatting cat-faced man pokes me, grunts, and speaks loudly to another man who peaks around him to look at me. Finally, they leave me as I was, climb into a canoe and paddle away. They're rapidly followed by the other canoes, and at the last moment, I'm hefted back into the canoe I rode in yesterday.

The man from the back of the canoe hands me food and drink, opens his mouth wide, and points at his tongue. Then he points at me. I nod in understanding as he and his partner push the canoe back into the river. Today I'm able to sit and watch the countryside pass by on either side of the river. It's a never-ending mass of trees, vines, and thick vegetation. The men seem to be able to move the canoe effortlessly despite the strong current. Their paddles strike the water in disciplined synchronization, keeping a steady but silent rhythm. This team of paddlers must spend a lot of time working in this fashion.

I think of my home and I wonder if I will ever return to it. How far away could it be? What direction would I take to get back there? I thought I was bored with my routine, but now I wish for the comfort of familiarity. I think of the six hundred and eighteen steps we carved in stone, steps that lead from the sea to the monastery at the summit. I think of the orange beaked, black and white puffins, which kept us company while we tapped away at the stone. Suddenly, the man behind me grabs my shoulder and shakes me from my thoughts about home. Again, he points into his mouth and I realize I have learned his word for *eat*. Then he tips his head back, makes gulping noises, and I learn another word: *drink*.

By the end of the day, I'm feeling much stronger. I begin to think of this man as my new guardian. The man at the front of the boat ignores me completely. I tire of watching the back of the man in front of me as he pulls the canoe up the river. I turn and face the man in the back. The paint on his face has lost its shine, and much of it has rubbed off. He has a kindly looking face that reminds me of Lector Beccán on a good day. I point at things, and he tells me their names. I enjoy the sound of his laughter when I say something wrong, but overall, I'm finding that I'm able to learn his language quickly. He seems to enjoy teaching me.

At the end of the day, I'm strong enough to climb from the canoe on my own. Initially, I find my legs wobble as I try to stand and walk. All around me, men are busy gathering wood for the fire. My contributions are meager, but I feel like the men around me appreciate that I'm joining in their collective efforts. I notice my teacher approach the cat-faced man who seems to be the leader of these men. When he turns to point at me, I realize that he and the cat-faced man are talking about me. As strange as they are to me, I must seem odd to them as well. Their conversation seems easy, and the masked man seems relaxed. I hope this means that I need not fear them, but I can't help being wary. I'm not used to spending time among large groups of people. I'm more used to talking to rocks.

After dinner, the sun sets and the men quickly go to sleep, leaving two men to stand watch. As I try to fall asleep, I run through the words I have learned, committing them to memory. After one day, I calculate that I have a vocabulary of twenty words in this new language.

My lessons continue over the next two days. I'm sure I could learn faster if my instructor didn't need to paddle. I wish I could know more about him and his people. It's one thing to learn random, isolated words, and quite another thing to be able to form sentences and complex thoughts. If I am to live among these people, I hope that I will spend time with this man. The others tolerate my presence, but otherwise don't seem interested in me.

The next morning as I begin practicing words, the man at the front of the canoe turns around abruptly and speaks angrily through tight, pinched lips. It seems that he has grown tired of hearing us talk. The moment he returns to a forward-facing position, he ducks swiftly. I should have ducked as well. A thick sticky mass of spider webs covers my face. I think of the giant spider that calls this mess home and I wonder if it is crawling around on my head or neck. The man from the front of the canoe turns and laughs. I have finally found a way to please him, I guess. The morning passes slowly. The river's path is half as wide as it had been several days earlier, and instead of following a straight line, it meanders around bends and turns. It had been easy to see the other five canoes at any given time. Now they are beyond our line of sight. Sometimes only the canoe in front of us is visible.

The current is more peaceful. I take a drink of water and the man at the back of the boat nods, encouraging me. These quiet people who paddle canoes remind me of the monks that raised me. In my entire life, I have not talked to more than five people. I moisten my lips and set down the hollow gourd. I wonder if we have been quiet for long enough that the man in the front of the boat might permit a brief lesson. I open my mouth to speak to the man in the back of the boat, hopeful to have even one new word to work on.

I hear a whirring sound. The eyes of the man at the back of the boat grow wide and his face opens up in shock. He falls forward and lands on my lap. An arrow protrudes from his back. I quickly swivel to look behind me. The man at the front of the boat has turned in our direction. His darting eyes seek the origin of the attack. A second arrow finds his heart and he falls into the water with a splash. I dive backward into the canoe, in an effort to protect my body with the sides of the canoe. I'm sweating, my heart is pounding, and I'm afraid of what comes next.

Shrieks fill the air. It sounds like animals dying. As I lay in the bottom of the canoe, fearful about what will happen, I wonder if I would have been better off if I had perished during the ocean storms.

Chapter 2

I wait in terror, cowering in the bottom of the canoe, expecting a spear to punch through my chest, or something even worse, though it is hard to imagine something worse than being speared to death. After what seems like an eternity, I am surrounded by canoes. On one side there is an older man, a terrifying woman about my age, and a boy that seems a couple of years younger than me. On the other side is a man about my age, and another younger boy. Their faces are painted deep red. For some reason, though less in number, these people seem more horrifying than the men I traveled with on the river. Perhaps because I have gotten a good look at how true their arrows fly.

They swiftly lead my canoe to the banks of the river. One of the men drags the lifeless body of my instructor from the boat, quickly separates the hair from the top of his head with a knife, and dances triumphantly around his body. I can't look upon the man's body. I'm glad that his partner fell into the water, and it looks like this enemy hasn't retrieved him from the river. I shiver at the thought of what they might do to me.

The young woman circles me while bent in a position from which she might strike, like I am a snake that might spring from a coil. I've never been this close to a fully dressed woman before, let alone a half-naked woman with wild eyes. I wish she would stop staring at me. Not knowing what else to do, I stretch my arms wide and tip my head back. A gesture which I think indicates that I accept my fate is in their hands.

The woman pokes my chest, as if to confirm my humanity. She turns to the older man and speaks quickly. A few words sound familiar. When she is done talking, they look back at me. I say the word I was taught for *river*, then I start telling my story in my language. They look at me strangely. It is clear they have never heard anyone speak in my native tongue. They tell me their names, and I'm careful to remember them. I think sharing names is a good sign that they don't intend to slay me. The older man is Spits Teeth. The warlike woman is Ferocious Wind. The young man holding the dead man's hair in his left hand pats his chest with his right hand and tells me his name is Black Rat Snake. I recognize the last part of his name from my lessons. It seems the enemies of this forest speak the same language. I pat my chest and tell them my name is Conchobar. The young man repeats the three syllables back to me, evenly and confidently. The others take turns repeating my name. The younger boys are named Fragrant and Earth Shakes.

The rest of the party has lifted their canoes and carried them down a trail that leads into the woods. I'm not certain, but I think the group whose names I know are a family unit. Spits Teeth points to the canoe they captured me in and tells me to carry it.

As we travel through the woods, the group makes frequent stops, gathering provisions along the way. I learn the names of plants and trees I've never seen before. They gather a lot of stringy bark and vines, and big globs of sticky sap the size of my fists.

The longer we travel, the heavier the canoe gets. My legs wobble and I stumble. The third time I trip, my canoe is given to the young boys to carry. Even so, I'm not able to keep up.

A couple of days of food and water have helped, but I'm still weak. I try to keep a steady pace until finally, I'm unable to continue.

There's a strange, dizzy, tingling feeling in my head. I feel myself sagging to the ground. My useless body has given out. I feel like I'm in a dream. I'm surrounded by color, shades of reds and pinks. I'm surrounded by moisture and I feel hydrated rather than parsed. I have a sense of calm. I feel my hands reach for a rope at the center of my belly. It's a familiar dream that comes to me often, but this time I'm stuck within the dream. I don't feel the need to escape it. I feel as if I might dissolve into it.

Suddenly, I'm doused with brisk spring water again. When I return to consciousness, I'm shocked to find myself lying in the dirt. My hooded robe has been removed. My travel companions are staring at my naked body. I manage to prop myself on my elbows and my mouth hangs open. I haven't seen my body since being rescued. My arms and legs are so thin, it hardly seems that any flesh lies beneath my skin. My stomach buckles beneath my ribcage which looks like it might collapse within itself. Black Rat Snake helps me to my feet. I'm handed a breechcloth and left alone with Black Rat Snake, who shows me how to put it on. My robe provides for modesty and warmth, but it's too much for a hot day of walking.

My travel companions stop to prepare camp for the night. In no time, they've created a comfortable covering overhead and a warm fire banked with stones to reflect heat toward the shelter. Ferocious Wind brings me a bowl of greasy soup. It tastes awful, but I can feel my body absorbing the fatty liquid. The rest of the group has continued ahead, only Spits Teeth and his family remain behind with me. I wonder why they are bothering with me. Am I a curiosity? Am I valuable in some way? Do they have something horrible planned for me in the future? I wish I could know.

Our early stop means that sunset is hours away. The family sits around the fire, and each has a knife and a chunk of wood in their hands, making something. Perhaps their survival depends on doing something of value every minute of every day. It reminds me of the

Abbey. From the moment I woke up until the moment I went to bed, it was always something—chiseling stone, tending the garden, thatching roofs, studying the Bible, or attending services.

Since I don't have anything to work on, I stand up and start collecting wood for the fire. Spits Teeth stands up, leans forward aggressively, wags his finger at me, and points to the fire. Rest. I nod, affirming that I understand. He adds a growl and I understand that I am expected to obey this man.

Although I don't have much experience with groups of people, I watch the family to see if I might understand them better, even if I don't know many of the words they speak. It appears the younger boys are telling stories, perhaps from the family's history. They are affable and seem to enjoy each other's company. The one named Fragrant appears to be a year or two older than the one called Earth Shakes. Fragrant laughs twice as much as Earth Shakes does, and Fragrant seems to look to Earth Shakes for approval rather than the other way around. Over and over again, he points to his behind, pinches his nose and waves his open hand in the air in front of his face. It seems the boy is known by two names, the milder Fragrant and the more specific name, Gassy Ass. Then they tell the story of the other boy's naming. Despite their extensive pantomime, I'm not certain why that boy is called Earth Shakes. It looks like he's trying to stand on the ground while shivering. Maybe he's always cold. I'm more and more certain that Fragrant and Earth Shakes are brothers.

The boys call upon the young woman to speak for a while. I understand a few of her words. The gestures they make help me understand some of the words I don't know. I guess that the girl is named for a big storm. I wonder if she was born during a storm, got lost during a storm like I did, or has a stormy temperament. Even when she's calm and at rest, there is something about her that seems wild, edgy, and poised to spring into action at a moment's notice. Strangely, the older man never seems to look in her direction, acknowledge her presence, or have any curiosity about what she's doing or saying. I've been among them for less than a day, but I've not seen him look at or speak to her even once, yet she seems to be everywhere.

Black Rat Snake stands by the fire. I already know the word for snake. He puts his hands together at the side of his head, tilts his head sideways, and shuts his eyes. I guess he means to convey sleeping. Then he holds his arm against his chest and gazes lovingly into the crook of his arm, rocking it back and forth, as if he is holding a baby. Then he motions back and forth with his arm in a repeating S pattern, like a snake would make slithering through the grass. Next, he makes a motion indicating the full length of the snake, from the ground to his chin—perhaps the big snake is five feet long. Finally, he conveys an exaggerated expression of surprise, several times in quick succession, and I'm guessing that he came to his name as a baby when the snake was discovered alongside him.

I look closely at Black Rat Snake and Ferocious Wind. Sometimes it is harder to tell whether brothers and sisters are related. I'm nearly certain that they are all children of Spits Teeth, therefore siblings. I wonder if it is unusual for young women to travel in the woods among men. In my life, I have seen very few women. Sometimes when I traveled with the monks to the big island to harvest thatch for our roofs I saw women from a distance, and those women didn't look anything like Ferocious Wind. I gaze down at myself, remembering how I'm dressed, and I have to admit that the men here look very different also. I think I prefer my robe, but it does get warm. It seems immodest and liberating at the same time.

With the sun setting, the spring air has chilled and I don my heavy robe again.

In the morning, I'm given another helping of fat soup, then I follow the family down the path to wherever it is they're going.

The younger boys have found something to squabble about.

They seemed to be getting along so well yesterday. Finally, their disagreement becomes loud enough to attract the attention of Spits Teeth. As the boys are about to knock each other with their fists, Spits Teeth saunters to their side, and with a hand on each boy's back, he smashes them into each other roughly, growls like an animal and nods his head toward the enemy's canoe. Whatever their disagreement, the boys run to carry the canoe down the trail.

A couple of hours later, Spits Teeth stops and points to a dark clearing in the woods full of fallen, rotting logs. The boys hurry into the clearing and gather small mushrooms in their pack baskets. Black Rat Snake follows Spits Teeth from the clearing. Ferocious Wind and I follow them twenty feet down the path to a wide creek. In a few minutes, Black Rat Snake produces a handful of beige grubs. Spits Teeth hooks a grub on a small bone hook tied to thin twine attached to a stick and drops it in the water.

Ferocious Wind squats above the river. Her hand darts into the water and she pulls out a small, crab-like creature. She flashes me a wild, toothy grin. I wonder if she plans to pop the crayfish in her mouth. Sometimes when she looks at me, I wonder what she is thinking. She holds the crayfish behind its pinchers for me to see, then puts it in a bag. She announces, "Crayfish." I follow her lead, plant my feet in the water, turn over rocks, and dash my hands under the water. My first catch has a tight lock on my pointer finger. I hold it up in the air, crinkle my nose and laugh. She hurries over, plucks the crayfish from my finger and puts it in her bag.

Half an hour later, the boys arrive at the river with their mushroom harvest and join in the crayfish hunt. It doesn't take us long to fill Ferocious Wind's woven bag. Spits Teeth has finished fishing, and grunts impatiently while the rest of us scamper from the creek. Spits Teeth has seven fat fish strung along a vine through their gills. He hands them to Black Rat Snake with a grunt and heads off down the trail. The rest of us hasten to catch up.

My companions' moods seem to be changing. I guess that we're nearing their destination. I wonder if this family lives alone in the wild woods, or whether they're part of a greater group of people, perhaps some sort of town or village. The thought of living amongst a large group of people worries me. I start to sweat and I feel my blood race through my body. With every step we take, the woods seem less dense. On one side of the trail, there is a steep, rocky decline. On the other side, the trees are well spaced out, and the deadfall beneath them is scant. In the distance, I hear voices, and the smell of woodsmoke is carried through the woods on a swift breeze. I wonder how many people live in this woodland village. I hope it's not too many.

A young woman with wild eyes and waving arms jumps out from behind a large tree. Though I know that it is Ferocious Wind, and somehow I understand that she is scaring me as some kind of joke, my legs buckle beneath me again. As I fall, I'm aware of my body hitting the ground. I also sense my body pitching toward the left and rolling until I feel my head thump into a rock.

Chapter 3

I feel a throbbing pain at the side of my head, and I feel dizzy, like I might fall down again, except I have the feeling that I'm floating. I'm aware of my red dream again, and the bond at the center of my belly. I wrap the fingers of both hands around the cord, and I feel a gentle, nudging tug at my core. I hear two men talking. They speak in the strange language I have been learning. Strangely, I understand every word, not just words here and there. I wonder how this is possible. Rapidly I blink my eyes, open them in a flutter, and see two men staring sympathetically at me. I'm laid out on some kind of table at chest level for the shorter man. They look into each other's eyes, then they look back at me. The taller man says, "Are you with us, boy?"

Though it hurts to move my head, I nod slightly. My head is swimming, and I'm confused. Is this man speaking my language, or do I now understand his?

The shorter man hurries off, talking as he works. "Something for swelling. Something for the poison. Something soothing. Something slippery. Something for the pain. Something for the itch."

The taller man addresses his partner. "Let's not forget something to drink and something to eat. This boy is emaciated, dehydrated, and malnourished, Gathers Seeds."

Gathers Seeds titters, tongue to teeth like a chipmunk, and

scurries about. He tells the taller man that there is soup beside the fire, then returns to his work. He unwraps each tiny woven bag, dropping pinches of their contents into a bowl. Then he smells the contents, tentatively at first, as if committing the combination of smells to memory. Then he grinds the contents together with a smooth rock and adds a generous amount of animal oil.

Soothingly, the taller man tells me that his name is Three Fingers. He explains that I have fallen and hit my head, and that they have examined my wounds, applied poultices and wraps, and that they think my head will be fine in a couple of days. He explains that Spits Teeth and Black Rat Snake brought me to them several days ago. In addition to hitting my head on a rock, I landed on a nest of ground bees. I've been stung hundreds, perhaps thousands of times. Three Fingers explains that bee stings are poisonous, some people are more sensitive to their poison, and even those that aren't sensitive to the poison can be affected when they're stung by that many bees. Three Fingers's lips have stopped moving, but still, I hear him talking. I'm amazed. How can I understand this man? Is he putting thoughts in my head? Sympathetically, Three Fingers says, "My biggest concern is how skinny you are. We can fix your head and heal your swelling, but it will take time to heal your body."

Three Fingers helps me sit and props a back brace on top of the elevated bed table. A warm, soft animal skin covers the brace and feels luxurious against the skin on my back. Then he holds a hollowed-out gourd to my lips and I take a sip of water. It reminds me of the men that found me on the riverbank beside the ocean. I thank Three Fingers and ask, "How is it I can understand you and your language?"

Three Fingers places a reassuring hand on my shoulder. "I have an uncommon ability. I can communicate, brain to brain. I also have a gift for language. I have taught you much and you learn quickly. It would seem you also have uncommon abilities. Now you must eat." I watch the man walk to the fire and scoop stew from a large ceramic pot into a small wooden bowl. A wooden spoon seems to appear in his hand. He feeds me a spoonful of the stew, and I swallow. It reminds me of the soup that Ferocious Wind brought me on the trail, only it tastes good, bursting with the flavor of mushrooms, something that tastes like onions, and seasonings I can't name or describe. "Gathers Seeds is a good cook, don't you think?" Three Fingers rubs the round belly on his otherwise tall and slender frame. I take a few swallows of the soup. Three Fingers vocalizes approval and begins humming—a slow and soothing song. After it repeats a few times, I find myself blinking slowly. Three Fingers wraps his arm around my back, removes the brace, and gently lowers me to the table.

When I awaken again, I am disoriented and I wonder how long I have been asleep. I see Three Fingers and Gathers Seeds holding hands, standing by the fire in the center of the building. I hear Three Fingers say, "His skin is hot. Very swollen. He needs to move. Sometimes he is not with us, yet he is not gone."

I try to speak, but I'm aware that I'm making more of a gurgling sound than forming actual words. Three Fingers and Gathers Seeds rush to my side.

Gathers Seeds opines, "We must take him to the lake. Sing to him." Three Fingers scoops me up in his arms without so much as a grunt. I feel like an infant. Three Fingers begins a quiet chant in a low, deep voice and follows Gathers Seeds through the doorway at the end of the building. My eyes are unaccustomed to the bright sunlight and I pinch them closed. When I try to open my eyes, it makes my head hurt, so I leave them closed instead.

After a short walk, Three Fingers squats at the edge of the water. He gently sets me down in the water, with my neck and head on the banks of the lake, and half of my body submerged in the shallow water at the edge of the lake. He carefully moves my arms and legs to a proper, extended position. I gaze into his face, and I have the feeling that I'm looking into the loving face of my mother, my mother, who died giving birth to me. A face I've never seen or can't remember. Three Fingers's song has grown louder, and it is soothing to listen to. It is a circular song, a song that ends just as it begins, then repeats. Even as he's singing, I hear him say, "You must fight this fever, Conchobar. We need you, my boy." I feel confused, I feel loved, and I feel the will to fight for my recovery.

Three Fingers remains by my side, with his knee in the water by my shoulder. His left foot cradles my head behind my neck. Gathers Seeds is standing in the water a short distance away, looking out into the lake, his arms crossed at his chest. Then he splashes over, squats by my side, takes my cheeks in his hands, and turns my head from side to side. He looks into my eyes from three inches away. With his finger and thumb, he opens my eyes even wider, and makes the sounds one makes when one is trying to solve a problem. He looks at Three Fingers and then hurries off into the woods. Ten minutes later, he returns, carrying some plant upside down, roots in the air. He dips the plant in the water and quickly washes away the dirt that remains tangled in its roots. Then he tells Three Fingers, "It has been long enough. Let's take him home."

On the way back to their home, I get my first look at their village. There are a dozen long houses arranged in a circle, within a fence of tall sticks around the perimeter. I see people buzzing around a fire in the middle, and darting in and out of doorways. There are many women, breasts uncovered, dressed in the same manner as Ferocious Wind was dressed, and swarms of toddlers and small children running around the village, naked, chasing each other. Three Fingers and Gathers Seeds's house is by far the smallest and is set off to the side from the others. As I'm returned to my elevated bed, I realize that Three Fingers is still singing his song. I take a deep breath and it crosses my mind that I feel better.

Moments later, Gathers Seeds places a huge bowl in Three Fingers's hands. Gathers Seeds says, "Cover him with this."

I don't know why I haven't noticed until now that Three Fingers has only two fingers on his right hand and one finger on his left hand. I'm very aware of his missing fingers as he rubs the salve on my body. It is a chunky green salve. It's slippery, soothing, and it smells like mint. It makes my skin tingle. When he is done, Gathers Seeds inspects his work. Then he looks at me and tells me that I will be cold when it dries. He gets a fur to cover me with. After having had a fever for so long, it is hard to imagine ever being cold again. Before Gathers Seeds returns with the fur, I'm shivering. He covers me with the thick black fur against my skin. Three Fingers tucks the edges under my body and explains, "Bearskin."

I've heard of bears, of course, but I have never seen one. Nor have I ever seen the skin of a bear. I close my eyes. I'm tired. It seems that all I do is sleep. I wonder how I could possibly still be tired. As I'm falling asleep, I think about these two strange men that hold hands, possess magical powers, and how comforting it is to be in their company. During my entire childhood, I don't remember ever being touched, nor do I remember seeing the other men on our island ever touch each other. After spending time in the care of these healers, I'm not sure whether it is stranger to be touched all the time, or whether it is stranger never to be touched.

I open my eyes. I am surrounded by people staring down at me. Gathers Seeds uncovers me and helps me sit up against the back brace. Three Fingers introduces my guests. They nod their heads as he says their names. I'm grateful that he also explains how they're related to one another. Fish Basket and Loon Feather are sisters, and wives of Spits Teeth. Fish Basket looks away as she's introduced and Loon Feather looks at her sister.

Three Fingers introduces Fish Basket's children. Black Rat Snake offers me half a smile, acknowledgment that we have met already. Ferocious Wind looks into my eyes as if she's not sure what I'll do, or what she'll do. Another girl named Fern is slightly younger than Ferocious Wind. Fern doesn't look directly at me, but she doesn't look away either. Fish Basket holds a baby girl named Smoky Shrew.

Loon Feather's oldest child is a daughter my age, a girl named Tends the Hearth. I've met her sons Gassy Ass and Earth Shakes. Three Fingers confirms that the boy was born during an earthquake that shook the ground as he was being delivered. As Loon Feather's youngest child is introduced, the 12-year-old boy begins to parade about the healer's longhouse, chest forward, hands upside down on his butt cheeks, stretching his neck and honking. That curious habit has properly earned him the name of Struts Like a Goose.

Three Fingers tells them my name and helps them practice saying it. I discover that Struts Like a Goose doesn't speak words. The family doesn't say much or stay long. Struts Like a Goose leads the way out. Ferocious Wind is the last one to leave. Before she exits, she assumes her wild, pouncing stance. She says, "Hurry up and get better so we can continue our adventures."

I answer, "Thank you, I will."

Big-eyed, she looks at Three Fingers. "He speaks our language?"

Three Fingers crosses his hands at his waist and nods. "Yes, I taught him."

She laughs wildly and springs through the doorway.

A couple of minutes later, an elderly woman shuffles through the doorway, wrapped in blankets. She is accompanied by a middle-aged man. Three Fingers introduces the ancient matriarch. Hole in the Roof has walked the earth for eight decades. The shaman, Dancing Bear, is three decades her junior. Three Fingers explains the significance of the matriarch and the shaman. The matriarch strokes my chest, runs her fingers through my hair, and mumbles sweetly. The shaman places a hand on each of my feet, offers a brief prayer and then they depart. When their visit is complete, the rest of the village passes through the healer's lodge. Gathers Seeds doesn't permit anyone to stay long. Three Fingers explains that Gathers Seeds had argued with Dancing Bear against allowing me to have visitors, but Dancing Bear insisted that everyone have a chance to meet me.

I ask Three Fingers why there are so few men in the village. Some are pursuing an enemy. Others are on a hunt. Many are working in the woods preparing wood for the winter, though it is only spring. Men don't spend much time within the village walls except during the winter season. There is so much to know about these people.

Gathers Seeds brings me another serving of stew. I feel like I've had ten meals a day since I have been in their care. I take a couple of bites, then look up and ask what will become of me once I'm healed.

Three Fingers answers, "I think you'll go to live with Spits Teeth as part of their family."

I repeat, "As part of their family?"

He answers, "Yes, they have adopted you."

I wonder why they would adopt me, and Three Fingers answers. Sometimes I forget that he can hear me even if I don't speak out loud. "They think you are good luck. They've never seen anyone that looks like you. You might have noticed you don't look the same as the rest of us do."

I look down in shame. "I'm not good luck. I am cursed."

Three Fingers asks, "Why do you think you are cursed?"

It is one of few facts about my family that I know. Lector Beccán told me that Fionán of Clonard brought me to the abbey. It would seem that my father cursed my mother and her offspring. I don't know much more than that. The only other thing I know about my mother is that she died when I was born and that her name was Rowsheen. Fionán brought me to the abbey so that I might survive and to hide me from my father. Lector Beccán did not believe in the curse, but I do. It seems that bad things happen to me all the time. Like getting lost at sea, for example. Or falling off the path and smashing my head and getting stung by bees. Bad things also happen to people around me, like the men in the canoe.

The healer places his hand on my shoulder and suggests that I look at it differently. "Don't you think it is miraculous that you survived being lost at sea? It would appear you have also survived falling off the path. The bees couldn't even kill you. And, has everyone you know been tragically killed?"

Three Fingers is convincing, but I'm still unsure. I want to believe him. I take a deep breath and try to finish my stew. I'm disappointed to know that I'll be living among a large family. I wish I could just stay in the healers' lodge, but I know that I'm in no position to make requests or demands. The one time in my life that I exercised my own discretion, I ended up lost at sea. I had better stick with doing what I'm told.

Chapter 4

After having spent several weeks with the healers, Gathers Seeds and Three Fingers agree that I'm healed. They think that I'm ready to move in with my adopted family, but I'm not so sure.

In a quiet moment, I ask Three Fingers what happened to his hand. Gathers Seeds looks up into the healer's eyes, touches his forearm briefly as if to reassure his partner, then begins to prepare a morning meal.

Three Fingers tells me about his childhood. The people of his birth live along the coast, way to the south. He speaks dreamily. "I used to enjoy watching out over the massive ocean. Its spirit still speaks to me, even from deep within the woodlands. Sometimes I lie awake at night thinking of the salty smelling air and the comforting sound of waves rhythmically rolling onto the shore. I remember walking across the sand, collecting seashells."

He tells me a story about being taken captive, along with two of his brothers, whom his captors slowly tortured and then killed. Three Fingers's chin drops to his chest. He tells me that it is still painful to think about, though it has been many years. A tear rolls down his cheek. I can't remember seeing a man cry, but I think his story might cause me to cry as well. Three Fingers concludes his story and tells me that I was lucky. Most captives, especially men, endure torture before being adopted, and many have fingers or toes hacked off.

I try to imagine hacking off somebody's finger. I think of my mallet and chisels. Masons often injure hands and fingers, but those are accidents. My mind wanders for a moment and I remember the years I spent working on the steps, up the island mountain to the abbey. I can't imagine hacking somebody's finger off on purpose. I shudder at the thought, and I feel Gathers Seeds's hand on my back. He places a wooden bowl in my hand. Then he brushes a stuck tear from Three Fingers's cheek.

It doesn't take long to prepare to move from the healers' lodge to Spits Teeth's longhouse. Aside from the breechcloth I was given, a knife, my robe, and a medallion that I have in a hidden pocket, I have no possessions. Even so, the healers fuss over my departure before they escort me to a longhouse at the back of the village.

Two women are kneeling at the entrance of the longhouse. I recognize Spits Teeth's wives, Fish Basket and Loon Feather. These sisters closely resemble one another. A finished pack basket sits beside each woman. Their fingers busily weave fibers through the frames of partially completed baskets in front of them. As we approach, Fish Basket's daughter, the one called Smoky Shrew, crawls into a finished basket that is lying on its side a few feet away.

Gathers Seeds tells Fish Basket to feed me as frequently as possible for the next ten days and to make sure that I drink as much water as possible. Three Fingers unwinds the bandages that they had tied to my head. Then he brushes away fragments of the yarrow that they used to cover my injury. Now that my hair has grown halfway to my shoulders, I doubt that anybody can see the injury on my head anyway. The women nod their heads and say as few words as possible, just enough to indicate that they have understood the healers' instructions. Neither woman takes her eyes from her work, and their hands continue weaving without pause.

As the healers walk away, I think of the silence that surrounded me at the abbey on the mountain. I'm going to miss the company of the friendly healers. I can't stop thinking about how Three Fingers and Gathers Seeds remind me of the quiet monks.

I stand in front of the women for several minutes, wondering what I should do. When the healers are completely out of sight, Fish Basket stands up from her work. She picks up one of the finished pack baskets and says, "You'll need this." She tells me to put it on, and then she adjusts the woven cords that go over my shoulder. The straps hold the basket in the proper position on my back.

Loon Feather stands up and says, "I have something for you also." She hands me a large hatchet made of stone tied to a wooden handle with thin strips of dried hide. Fish Basket takes my robe from me, places it in my basket, then the women lead me into the forest.

Twenty minutes later, we arrive in a clearing where men and boys are chopping away at logs. I recognize Fragrant and Earth Shakes at the same time they recognize me. They trot to my side, each boy takes one of my hands, and they lead me to the tree they're working on. I glance behind me, wondering if I should say anything to the women that brought me here, only to see them disappearing up the trail. I also see Struts Like a Goose, who darts around the clearing breaking twigs and filling pack baskets.

My arms haven't been used for a long time, but my muscles quickly remember working with the mallet. Chopping logs into firewood feels familiar. I enjoy watching the splinters fly from the blade of the hatchet and I think of the chips of stone dislodged by my chisel. After being away from home for so long, it is reassuring to be doing something that feels familiar.

Hours later, Earth Shakes tells me that it's time to go home. Each of the boys hefts a pack basket onto his shoulders, and, with as much wood as they can carry in their arms, they head back down the path toward home. Struts Like a Goose leads the way, honking triumphantly, signaling the end of the workday.

I'm amazed how big the longhouses are, and how they're able to stand. They look like they're built from bark and twigs because they are. Granted, there is a structure of stronger, thicker wood beneath. I think of the stone structures that make up the abbey complex, and I imagine they'll last for hundreds, perhaps thousands of years. I wonder, how long a house constructed of firewood can last?

On the island, some of the stone buildings were dome-shaped, made of stacked stones, cut to fit together precisely. Other stone buildings were just walls, and each summer, new thatching was strapped on top. I guess the new bark and twigs on the longhouses works the same, and I wonder how many layers of thickness are woven onto the longhouses. As I duck my head to enter, I also wonder whether they're able to keep out the rain.

Inside, there are pairs of bunks stacked along the outer walls and a wide aisle runs down the middle. I'm assigned a bunk at the top level, nearest the wall, next to Black Rat Snake. Ferocious Wind and Fern's bunks are just beneath. Fish Basket and Spits Teeth occupy the bottom-most bunks. Loon Feather and her children occupy the bunks across the aisle.

There's a circle of stones in the middle of the aisle between the compartments. A ceramic pot sits at the edge of the fire. Tends Hearth uses a large wooden ladle to fill bowls and Fish Basket scrapes something crunchy made from corn from a flat rock at the side of the fire.

Loon Feather's boys banter continuously while they eat. In between bites, I ask Fern where the others are. She explains that Spits Teeth, Black Rat Snake, and Ferocious Wind are on a raid, just as they were on a raid when they found me. I notice Fish Basket gently stroking her round belly while Fern talks. Fern is a pretty girl, two years younger than me and one year younger than her sister. Unlike the older women, Fern is not afraid to look into my face when we talk to each other. She is easygoing like the healers, and not wild-looking, like Ferocious Wind.

Fern asks me if I'd like to go fishing with her in the morning. I nod my head and ask if I'm allowed. "Don't I have to chop wood tomorrow?" Fern asks her mother, and her mother agrees that it would be permissible, so it is decided. It felt good to chop wood, but my body is sore from lack of use.

It crosses my mind that I intended to go fishing that fateful morning when I was swept away from my home. Memories of being lost at sea are never far from my thoughts. I don't know how many days I spent on the ocean before I was rescued. The thought of fishing with Fern causes me to recall a particular day on the water. It was a calm day at sea. Something was floating on the surface of the ocean. I put it on my hook, and I dropped my line in the water. Somehow I caught a fish. I remember eating it alive—every last bit of it except for the bones. If it hadn't been for that fish, I probably would have died. Thinking of those hungry days while I eat the food that Tends Hearth prepared, I'm grateful for this meal. I often try to remember how long I was adrift. Maybe there were twenty days before the fish and twenty days after. I keep replaying those days in my mind, trying to put the pieces together. I know I can't change anything about the way things happened, but replaying the events helps me accept my fate.

Shortly after everyone has eaten, Fish Basket hands me some furs and tells me they are for my bunk. I climb the rungs up the ladder made from saplings and lay the furs out. I lie on my back enjoying the softness and I try to think of how many people are sleeping in this one building. I'm tired, and I know I would normally fall asleep quickly, except for the fact that a girl is sleeping just a few feet away from me. I'm looking forward to going fishing and I enjoy talking with her, but my thoughts become scrambled when

I'm around Fern or Ferocious Wind. It was easier to think chaste thoughts when I lived on a sparsely populated island surrounded by monks. I know the monks wouldn't approve, and I know I shouldn't think such thoughts, but being surrounded by half-dressed girls my age makes my head spin. Despite my impure thoughts and the unfamiliar sound of people sleeping all around me, I'm finally able to fall asleep.

I feel a hand grab my elbow and shake me. I'm aware that I have been dreaming, the red dream again, only this time the cord was pulling me from the salty ocean and dropping me on the banks of the wide, brown river. It's very early, well before sunrise, and Fern is quietly telling me that it's time. I follow her down the ladder and we tiptoe from the longhouse. She has bone hooks, twine, wooden rods, and a large net made from woven vines. I have a knife and my new pack basket.

We head down the trail toward the lake. It's still dark when we reach a small clearing in the woods on the north side of the large lake. I use a flat rock to dig for worms in the soft loamy soil, and Fern turns over rocks and logs looking for grubs. Then we're off to the lake.

There's a boulder at the shore. The rising sun is at our backs. There is no wind, no breeze, and the surface of the lake is perfectly calm, except for the ripples left by fish jumping to catch insects. The fish are biting. We glance at each other, and Fern nods eagerly. I wonder who will catch the first fish. I hand her a worm and she gives me a grub. I poke a hook through the grub and tie the line to a stick. I tie a third hook with a worm and toss the hook out as far from the rock as I can. I glance at Fern and she is staring, intently watching her line.

We don't have long to wait. Two minutes later, Fern is patiently drawing the line in toward her, hand over hand until the flopping fish is splashing near the shoreline. I hand Fern my line and jump off the rock into the water with the net, just in time. The fish has managed to dislodge the bone hook from its mouth but can't escape the net. I return to the rock and bash the fish on the head just as Fern is pulling in another large fish on my line. I jump back into the lake with the net. I'm aware of my rumbling belly. Trout have become my favorite meal.

Several smaller fish follow the two large ones. Others from the village begin to arrive and take up positions along the shoreline. The hungry fish seem to be keeping all the children busy, and it would seem that everyone in the village will be well fed today.

The fish are still biting, but our worm supply is running low. Fern tells me that she will go get more as I bait the last worm on my hook. "I'll catch up with you when this worm is gone," I tell her. She smiles, nods sweetly, and is gone. I'm glad to have such a pleasant girl for a sister. I think it will be helpful to remind myself that she is my sister, as frequently as possible.

After a couple of minutes, I pull in my line, only to discover that my worm has been expertly nibbled from my hook by some crafty fish. I concede that worm to the fish. No matter, we have a hefty haul in our basket already. I dip the basket full of fish in the lake to keep them fresh, grab my digging rock, and set out to find Fern at the clearing in the woods.

As I round the bend in the trail that opens up into the clearing, I hear Fern scream. Then I see an enormous oak tree fall. The sound of her bones crunching under the weight of the ancient tree is lost within the overall collective explosion of the limbs and branches smashing into the ground. I am stunned. Conflicted. Should I see if she is merely injured? Perhaps I can help her. Should I run for help? Somebody will know what to do. I run toward the fallen tree. I see some of her hair from under the tree but I can't recognize anything that looks like her body. I take off, running as fast as I can.

When I get to the longhouse, I can't find anyone. Then I run to the healer's lodge. I grab Three Fingers's hand and pull him toward the doorway. "You must hurry. A tree has fallen on Fern." Gathers Seeds is right behind us as we race back to the clearing. When we arrive at the scene, Three Fingers circles the fallen tree, shaking his head, slowly. He looks at Gathers Seeds. Glumly, he pushes his lower lip forward. I find the spot where we can see Fern's hair, point, and holler. Three Fingers rushes to my side, kneels, and straightens the strands of black hair that stick out beyond the edge of the tree trunk.

I feel like I might cry. I imagine the pretty girl's face smashed into dirt beneath the weight of the colossal tree. How could this happen? One minute, Fern is standing in the clearing. The next minute, she is flattened beyond recognition.

Three Fingers asks me for my knife. I have to look away as he slices through her hair. He quickly puts Fern's hair in his pocket and gives me back my knife. Then he nudges me back down the path toward the village. Gathers Seeds makes a side trip to the lake to pick up the basket full of fish, and quickly catches up with us.

Fish Basket and Loon Feather have returned from wherever they had gone. Three Fingers places his hands on Fish Basket's shoulders. "Fern has been killed by a falling tree in the clearing near the lake. I'm so sorry." He lets go of her shoulders and puts Fern's hair in her hand. "This is all that remains."

Fish Basket turns into the arms of her sister, sobbing. I wish I were anywhere but here. Three Fingers turns toward me. "Get the men and boys from the woods. Tell them to bring their hatchets." I hurry away from the grieving women and run down the path into the woods. I feel so bad. I haven't known Fern very long. The people in this village have known Fern their whole lives, yet I do feel like I've lost a member of my family. Then I think of the kind man in the canoe who fell into my lap with an arrow in his back, and I gasp for air. It's the curse again. This time it has killed Fern. Instead of getting the men, I feel like I should run away into the woods. How else can I rid this village of the curse that follows me wherever I go?

I hear Three Fingers's voice in my head. *You are not cursed. Sometimes bad things happen. We can't know why, but we must go on. This is not your fault. Get the men and the boys.* I want to believe the voice, but I don't. Still, I obey.

Three Fingers leads the army of woodsmen to the clearing. Dozens of sharp, stone hatchets chop noisily at the ancient oak tree. After a while, the strikes fall into a rhythm, as one woodsman after another sets their pace with that of their family, friends, and neighbors. By the end of the day, they have retrieved the remains of the young girl. What little remains is wrapped and carried back to the village. Industrious women and children scurry back and forth with the wood from the fallen tree.

When we return to the longhouse at dusk, Loon Feather serves the fish for dinner. Fish Basket is buried beneath the blankets on her bunk. She alternates between whimpers and sobs. I lie in my bunk, several feet above. Tears stream down my face. I try to imagine how Fish Basket must feel. If she only knew about my curse. I feel like I pushed the tree down on Fern myself. That voice returns to my head, trying to talk me out of feeling guilty.

Fish Basket barely leaves her bunk the next day. I see her once or twice. She wears her daughter's salvaged hair. It is tied tightly at either end, braided, and bent back upon itself, so none can be lost. It hangs from a rawhide string around her neck and rests between her breasts. I surmise that she must wish to feel Fern's hair on her skin.

Three days have passed and now, Fish Basket is mourning again. While we worked in the forest today, she lost the baby that she was carrying. It's hard to watch her cry endlessly. Her daughter is dead, her baby is lost, and her husband and oldest children are away. I feel like it is my fault. I imagine Spits Teeth in a rage, furious about the loss of his young daughter and unborn child. I feel sorry for my adopted siblings and I grieve on their behalf while they are away.

Chapter 5

Months later, in the dead of winter, I'm still thinking about the missing member of our family. I wish people would talk about her from time to time. Except for the braid that Fish Basket wears on her chest, it's as if Fern never existed.

I'll never forget the day that Spits Teeth returned from raiding the enemy's villages. He returned with Black Rat Snake, Ferocious Wind, and fifteen warriors, two weeks after the tree killed his daughter. When he was told about Fern's death he shrugged it off, and the news of the loss of Fish Basket's baby registered even less of a response from him. Perhaps he feels grief without expressing it. Rather than consoling his family, he turned away.

The return of the raiding party was cause for celebration. At the large fire in the center of the village, the raiding party bragged about their exploits and reenacted their heroic deeds. The raiding party showed off piles of stolen furs, several fine-looking canoes, and a couple of well-constructed cook pots. They had burned a building in the enemy's village and three of the enemy were killed as evidenced by the scalps that were displayed. A miserable looking captive was tied to a post, awaiting his fate. On the way back, the party had hunted successfully and venison was plentiful. After the village feasted, the warriors slayed the captive. Then everyone danced to the beat of a dozen drums for hours. Everyone participated in the celebration, from the 80-year-old matriarch to the youngest child. I guess a war chief is expected to be fierce.

It's a cold winter's day. The wind is howling outside the longhouse. Snow is rapidly accumulating, adding to the two feet of snow which has piled up from back-to-back storms last week.

Spits Teeth, Black Rat Snake, Ferocious Wind and I are crafting weapons around the fire in the center of the longhouse. Spits Teeth efficiently chips away at flint stones with a round, fist-sized hammerstone, then he sculpts arrowheads from the chips with a pointy antler fragment. He easily maintains a pace of five arrowheads an hour.

A few days earlier, I began working on a Y-shaped maple log, twenty-five inches long. At the thickest point, just before the main trunk splits at the joint, the log is thicker. I painstakingly work at creating a perfectly round ball at what will become the deadly end of the club. As I work, I try to imagine swinging the club and cracking an enemy's skull with it. Perhaps if I think about it frequently, it will not seem so difficult when I actually have to do it. I think of my upbringing, the tranquil monks on my far-away island, and I wonder if I'll ever be able to fight alongside these people in this new land. I fear that they will turn on *me* if I don't.

Black Rat Snake is in the final stages of smoothing the handle of his club. He blows off a little dust, then smoothly runs the tip of his fingers up and down the shaft of the club. It is perfect. He sets the finished club down beside him. Then he puts his hands together in front of him.

Slowly, Black Rat Snake stretches his arms high above him. He bends and twists his body from side to side, releasing energy from sitting for too long, bending, stretching and yawning. He jumps to his feet, squats, then jumps into the air. He swings like a possum, only much faster, from the beams in the longhouse. He traverses the rectangle of the family's compartment, twenty feet long and twelve feet across. We count the laps together out loud. His arms give out at thirty and he bows proudly. It's a new record. Then he returns to the tedious weapon-making work by the fire.

Ferocious Wind also works on crafting a war club of her own. Spits Teeth doesn't seem to notice that her club looks identical to her brother's, he only seems to notice Black Rat Snake's accomplishments. I can't remember seeing him speak to her. He doesn't seem to care what she does. At least he doesn't seem to care that she spends all of her time among the men and boys. I wonder how long she has accompanied them on hunting trips and raids. I must admit that she scares me, yet I can't help but look at her every chance I get.

Despite the fact that it is winter, everyone is busy. Fish Basket and Loon Feather work beside the fire, twisting thin strips of cedar bark into strong, thin strands of cordage. They have baskets full of material to process, and an enormous mound of completed string piled up beside them. Fragrant and Earth Shakes busily whittle wooden bowls and utensils. Struts Like a Goose's whittling only yields woodchips. Smoky Shrew plays among the woodchips on the floor. Tends Hearth prepares dinner, stirs the pot, feeds the fire, and looks for opportunities to criticize. Many times I have seen her try to lure Ferocious Wind away from working with the men and boys. When Tends Hearth becomes too annoying, Ferocious Wind discourages her by making scary faces and wild animal noises.

Black Rat Snake begins work on another new club. The beginning part is his favorite. Chips of wood fly everywhere as he chisels large chunks from the log. It feels like he is making fast progress, and the log quickly begins to take the shape of a club, thin enough at one end to fit his hand perfectly, thick enough at the other end to dispatch the hardest headed enemy at the killing end of the club.

Spits Teeth takes a minute between arrowheads to examine our work. He grunts approval at Black Rat Snake's pace. Then he admonishes me, wagging his first finger in front of my face. "You must remove larger chucks at this stage. You are not ready for that finishing work yet. Are you going to spend all winter making one club? Black Rat Snake is already making his third. Is there anything you are good at, boy?" He grunts. I think of Spits Teeth's long, frequent absences between spring and autumn, and I miss those departures. Winter seems to last forever.

I bite my cheek and nod submissively. Obediently, I slice out larger chunks of woodchips. Working with wood is very different from working with stone. I wish I could work faster. I can feel anger boiling behind my eyes and I mash my molars together hard, determined not to cry tears of fury, like a child. Sure, the others have had many more years of experience making weapons in the winter, but it still rankles to be rebuked. My next tap is way too strong. Why have I let my mind drift off? Why have I struck in frustration, or was it anger? The club is ruined. I drop my forehand into my hands, knowing I must start all over again.

Spits Teeth yells at me, both hands swinging out in front of his body. I mutter my apologies. From the corner of my eye, I see Fish Basket wince and turn away. Ferocious Wind briefly looks at me. She knows how I feel when her father berates me. I wish it didn't happen so often. Spits Teeth scowls, retrieves another Y-shaped log, and drops it in front of me before returning to making arrowheads. I take a deep breath, pick up the new log, and watch Black Rat Snake for a moment. I must try harder to copy his methods and coax a war club from this new chunk of wood. The idea comes to me to make Black Rat Snake a club with a snake's head at the end of the club, over the ball.

Twenty minutes later, Tends Hearth proclaims that dinner is ready. Winter soup can be thin, not much more than oily water, with some corn and dried beans and, if we are lucky, some ground spices.

Dinner provides a brief break. Spits Teeth dominates the conversation, running down a list of what we've made, and what he expects we'll need to accomplish before spring. I find myself wondering how many war clubs, tomahawks, spears, knives, bows, and arrows we'll need to match similar weaponry surely in the process of being made around the hearth fires of our enemies.

Spits Teeth details his plans for the summer, telling us that he will drive our enemies away. My mind wanders as I watch instead of listening. Despite repeating his plans over and over, almost on a daily basis, the intensity of Spits Teeth's hatred never diminishes. The enemy speaks the same language. They live in the same kind of lodgings and cultivate the same crops. They hunt the same game. They use the same tools and weapons. Why must they be enemies? The bitter rivals seem destined to destroy each other. I look at the weapons all around us. It seems there are enough to kill every member of the enemy's village. Twice.

Finally there is silence. Dinner is over, and Spits Teeth has finished talking. I ask, "How will we defeat Bobcat Mask?"

The question seems to please him. He says, "We must sneak up on them. We'll slither into their village, just like the big old snake that slithered into my son's bed when he was a baby. Then we'll sting them with all of these weapons, just like those bees stung you when you arrived in our village."

For several years, Spits Teeth has been trying to convince everyone to attack the enemy. Not just skirmishes back and forth, but an all-out assault. A total annihilation. Each year, his impassioned plea garners more and more support. Splits Teeth tries to remind them of a glorious victory from many years earlier.

After dinner, Spits Teeth works on crafting knife blades. We return to working on our clubs. The women work on a large fishnet, tying the cordage into diamond-shaped knots. Tends Hearth sweeps woodchips and adds them to a basket that she frequently uses to stoke the fire.

It's hard to believe that I've been in this village since spring, and now it is the middle of winter. Maybe it has been three hundred days, and still I can't get used to sleeping among piles of people. I'm always the last to fall asleep. I try to ignore the sounds of Spits Teeth roughly coupling with his wives, or the whimpering sounds his wives make afterward. I can't imagine I could sleep through such sounds even if I spent thousands of days in this longhouse. When Spits Teeth falls asleep, it feels like the longhouse is shaking from the noise he makes. It isn't just Spits Teeth's snoring that keeps me awake. It seems like the sound of snoring surrounds me. It should be possible to fall asleep with my fingers pressing my ears closed, but I haven't been able to manage it so far.

A smoldering anger builds within me. I try to push away thoughts of Spits Teeth shouting at me. I'm not accustomed to being admonished. I repeatedly replay his harsh words in my head. "Is there anything you are good at, boy?" It's hard to fall asleep when you're angry.

Then I start to hear chattering. Instead of trying not to hear, now I'm trying to make sense of the change around me. The snoring has stopped. Is it a quiet conversation between two members of the family? I listen intently.

One after another, I hear the various family members talking in their sleep, only I can't understand a word that anyone is saying. One mumbles. Another grunts in response. It is like they are having a conversation.

The bunks shudder and the walls shake. I want to get away as fast as I can. Unfortunately, I have to carefully crawl across Black Rat Snake's sleeping body to descend from the elevated bunk. Despite shaking in fear, I'm able to cross my brother's body without waking him. As I reach the ground, the sounds grow louder. I feel an urgency to get away, yet I have lost control over my body. It is like a nightmare from which I cannot wake.

Previously the strange sleep talking consisted of muted

mumblings. It has now elevated to a feverish pitch. They yell and scream at each other, even the ones who normally cower in fear. I stand in the aisle near the hearth fire, and I can see the sleeping family, on both sides of the aisle. I can't understand how they can sleep through whatever is happening. My head aches, and I feel dizzy.

I wonder if it is *them* or if it is *me*. Then I wake up. I recognize that I've had a bad dream, yet I'm not completely sure it was all in my imagination.

Chapter 6

It doesn't come to me every night, but my new nightmare returns far too often. Every time it happens, I'm terrified for hours after I wake up. Now that it has happened a third time, I need to talk to somebody about it. I trudge to the healer's lodge and find Three Fingers there. I tell him about my nightmares. He listens carefully and asks questions.

Three Fingers thinks that my dream is a result of all of the trauma that I've experienced in the last year, and the rapid changes that I have been experiencing. The shock of going from spending hardly any time among people to never having quiet moments to myself may also be a part of it.

I'm not sure that he's right. I ask him if he thinks it has anything to do with the curse. He discounts the notion that I am cursed and makes suggestions for where I can go to find tranquil moments from time to time. Though we have discussed the curse before, Three Fingers doesn't seem to mind me bringing it up again.

Six weeks hence, late winter has given way to early spring. The equinox is fast approaching, yet the air is still cold.

Before anyone else is awake, Fragrant bundles up in his warmest clothes, climbs to the top bunk, reaches clumsily across Black Rat Snake and shakes my shoulder. I wake with a start, shivering in fear, but glad to have escaped my vexing nightmare. Our brother grumbles angrily at the disturbance, rolls over, and goes back to sleep.

Outside the longhouse, we strap snowshoes on our feet, grab our hunting gear, and optimistically put empty pack baskets on our backs. Fragrant is in a talkative mood as we walk across the frozen surface of the lake.

Sometimes it is hard to believe that he is the same age as Ferocious Wind. Maybe because she is serious and determined, whereas Fragrant is fun-loving and irreverent. At first, I concluded that he was a boy of many words and few thoughts. Perhaps I judged him based on the fact that he is usually accompanied by Struts Like a Goose, and must speak for both of them. Lately as I've been watching more closely, I've begun to think that Fragrant might be smarter than he pretends to be.

This morning, Instead of jumping from topic to topic, he sticks to a subject that makes me most uncomfortable. "Do you want to marry my sister?" The way he asks, it doesn't seem as though he would object. I'm glad that I don't need to respond to his question, as he quickly goes on to talk about all the women he'd like to spend time with. At first I'm not certain what he means when he tells me that he'd like to put his arrow in the quiver of a particular maiden in a neighboring village. I'm not accustomed to hearing such euphemisms.

He is unabashedly precise about his urges, and I can feel my cheeks redden. At the same time, I'm interested to hear what he has to say. Being raised by old monks who speak more about what happens when you sin than they do about the sinning itself, I know very little about the subject of coupling. Someday I'd like to put what I'm hearing to good use. For a couple of years, I've been experiencing urges of my own. However, I'm not imaginative enough to have contemplated all of the details that Fragrant so readily describes.

When we finally reach the opposite shore of the big frozen lake, it is still very early in the morning. On one hand, I am relieved that Fragrant has gone silent. On the other hand, I wonder whether there is still more that it would be helpful for me to know. For now, it is time to focus on the reason we are here.

We plan to hunt in an enormous meadow where the snow tends to be less deep than in other places. Its exposure to the strong north wind has left the tall dry grasses more accessible to wildlife during the cold winter.

Fragrant looks at me and puts his index finger to his lips, indicating that we should be quiet, and swings his head toward a game path that heads directly west. We have our bows in our right hands, with arrows at the ready, resting on undrawn bowstrings. We need to be ready to seize upon any opportunity that presents itself.

I wish that I had spent more time practicing. Fragrant quietly tells me that I couldn't hit a mountain if it were ten feet away. It sounds like a challenge and a joke at the same time.

Half an hour up the trail, we crest a small hill, traverse around a corner, and see a rabbit on a rock nibbling on a small clump of dried grass. Instinctively, Fragrant draws his bow and sends an arrow flying. The arrow lands in the grass the rabbit had been nibbling on. The rabbit is long gone.

Twenty minutes further up the trail, I send an arrow after a scurrying woodchuck. It moves faster than my arrow and easily manages to escape.

Now it's mid-morning and I'm beginning to think that our hunt will prove fruitless. The sun has dried the clumps of brown grasses, melting the frost from the tops of the fronds. The trail turns toward the north. An hour further up the trail, the terrain grows steeper and the trail passes among large boulders. We creep slowly through the boulders, carefully peeking around them. We haven't seen a single deer all morning. Normally, we would have expected to see deer far off in the distance, plentiful as they are. Finally, our luck turns.

At the top of the rocky hill, two deer are eating from a large patch of grass. Fragrant's arrow takes down the one on the right, and my arrow hits the one on the left. I quickly send a second arrow in behind the deer's ear, deep into its head. It drops to its knees and sags to its side. Even though the deer are very close, I'm nevertheless amazed that I have been able to kill one.

Fragrant looks at me with what appears to be a mixture of surprise and respect and slaps my shoulder. I laugh awkwardly. Though I'm a year older, my adopted brother is behaving like a worldly uncle as we make our way to the kills.

He drops to his knees and places both hands on the rib cage of his deer and he motions for me to do the same. He explains his ritual as he performs it. "We must give thanks to the Great Spirit for allowing our hunt to be successful. We express our appreciation, acknowledging that our existence depends on the generosity of our creator." Again, I'm surprised by Fragrant's words, deeds, and spirituality. Until today, I had not realized that he had such depth of character, and I wonder if others in the village know how intelligent and complex he is.

When our prayers are finished, Fragrant grins at me proudly and readies his knife for butchering. Moments later, we have painted each other's bodies with the wet blood of our kills. Our empty baskets will be full for our return trip. My mouth waters. I can almost taste the meat. I'm ready for some venison after what seems like an endless diet of lima beans, corn mash, and grease soup.

We finish the butchering by early afternoon. Our packs are loaded and ready to carry home. Fragrant suggests a quick side trip. Just ahead, there is a river. Before I consent to explore it, he is halfway there.

When I catch up, Fragrant is attempting to pick up a big rock. He can move it but not lift it. I jump in to help, and between us, we lift it from the ground. He says, "On the count of three." We swing the rock back and forth as he counts out loud and we let the rock fly. It crashes through the ice at the edge of the river and makes an explosive sound, leaving a hole in the ice much larger than the rock's diameter. The ice around the hole cracks, sending zig-zagged lines across the ice, radiating from the hole where the rock has landed. "Again," shouts Fragrant. We find another rock and send it flying through the ice.

After we fling a third rock, he jumps to the ice at the side of the river. He lays on his stomach and drinks water from the big hole he has made. He says, "I wonder if there are any fish in here that want to be caught today." He scurries back to his pack basket full of butchered deer and returns with some bone hooks, wound cordage, and little bits of deer intestines.

By mid-afternoon, Fragrant has grown tired of trying to catch fish. We have a long trip home with heavy baskets. He challenges, "I'll race you," and almost as fast as he says it, his feet begin moving.

His feet fail to grip the slippery surface of the ice, and Fragrant's body pitches forward into the water through the giant hole and makes a noisy splash. His arms flail and he tries to plant his feet on the bottom of the fast-moving river beneath him. In a matter of seconds, his desperate attempts to rescue himself have failed. The strong current sweeps him under the surface of the ice.

Horrified, I run down the side of the river, trying to keep up with the current. I see the panicked look on his face as his body slips beneath the icy surface, and I see his body disappear downstream. I can't move fast enough. I search the river's edge all the way to where it empties into the lake. There are plenty of places in the middle where there is open water. Fragrant might be able to jump out there if he doesn't drown before reaching those places—or if his head hasn't smacked against rocks or ice.

I search for another hour, though I know I am searching in vain. I conceal my basket beneath some hastily chopped pine boughs and heft Fragrant's basket to my back. It is a long, sad trip home.

I dread having to tell Fragrant's story. Spits Teeth's people are proud to hear stories of brave fallen warriors who valiantly dispatch enemies before succumbing heroically. This will not be such a story. Though I have never met her, I think of the young woman in the neighboring village. I wonder if she knows that he pined for her. I'm crushed by the thought that she will never know the man that might have become her husband.

When I return to the longhouse alone, I give the day's details. Just the facts. We walked across the lake. We saw a rabbit and missed. We saw a woodchuck and missed. We each took a deer. We threw rocks into the ice at the edge of the river. We tried but didn't catch any fish. Then Fragrant slipped, went under the ice, and disappeared beneath the surface.

Tends Hearth exclaims, "Couldn't you grab his hand before he went under?"

I hang my shaking head and explain that he was beyond my reach.

She wags her first finger at me and admonishes, "Couldn't you follow him down the river and pull him out there?" It seems to me that she thinks I killed Fragrant myself, on purpose.

I shake my head from side to side. My cheeks feel hot. Guilt and shame register in my brain and I'm angry with myself for not finding some way to save the boy, or at least prevent his reckless behavior on the ice. "I tried as hard as I could to find where he went under. I couldn't find him under the ice, and I couldn't find him down the river."

I feel the burning, accusatory gaze of the girl and it burns a hole into my consciousness. I try to think of what I could have done differently. I can't think of anything. I try to think about how I might have stopped the boy from going to the river, though he was insistent. When Tends Hearth buries her sobbing face in her open hands, I feel even worse.

The moon is full and the weather holds. A dozen men and boys head out into the night, on the slight chance that Fragrant might be rescued or found. I lead them across the lake and up the trail to the place we butchered the deer, then I lead them to the riverside. The haunting look on Fragrant's face, followed by his body getting sucked into the hole and down the river, loops continuously in my brain.

Fragrant is neither rescued nor recovered.

Chapter 7

The world is coming alive and the vibrant green reminds me of my home across the ocean. One night at dinner, Ferocious Wind says, "Conchobar, I'm going to turn you into a warrior." She nods her head for emphasis. "That's right, we start tomorrow."

I wish she had told me this privately. Tends Hearth laughs loudly and rolls her eyes. I'm pretty sure she doesn't believe that I can be a warrior. Maybe she doesn't believe in Ferocious Wind's ability to coach me. I already know what Tends Hearth thinks about Ferocious Wind being a warrior.

Black Rat Snake asks Spits Teeth if it is a good idea. Spits Teeth shrugs. Maybe he feels the same way Tends Hearth does. The war chief answers, "There's no warrior in that boy."

Ferocious Wind says, "He shall become a warrior, just you wait and see."

If she said she would teach me how to be a fish, I'd probably jump in the lake.

She warns me, "You'd better get a lot of rest tonight because tomorrow's going to be rough."

The next morning, we start with a swim across the lake. Then we run around the perimeter of the clearing. After we swim back across the lake we lift heavy logs to our shoulders. Ferocious Wind brags that she can do more squats than I can. I do my best to prove her wrong and fail. After a brief break, we return to the longhouse and she challenges me to catch her if I can. She climbs to the rafters and travels the perimeter of the compartment, Black Rat Snake's favorite workout. I jump, grab hold, and swing, hand over hand, as fast as I can go, trying to catch her. Tends Hearth stands below, hands on her hips, telling us that we are wasting our time. After three trips around the perimeter, my arms tire and I drop. The rest of the day is full of similar tasks which are to become our routine.

Six weeks later, both of us are stronger. I'm amazed at my transformation, and I'm able to make it twenty-five times around the perimeter of our living quarters before my arms give out. Recently, we've added weapons to our routine. The war clubs we made during the winter are put to use smashing punky, rotting stumps and trees. Ferocious Wind tells me that I must get used to the feeling of swinging the club and that I must know what it feels like when the club connects with a target. We spend endless hours flinging knives, throwing hatchets, and launching arrows into targets. She emphasizes, "You have to be better at this than the enemy. In a battle, it's them or you. Life or death. If you fail, one of our comrades dies. A wife loses a husband. A family loses a provider. You must not hesitate. You must *defeat* them."

One midsummer day, Ferocious Wind announces that she is taking me on a hunting trip. She wants me to practice on moving targets. Tends Hearth protests Ferocious Wind's plan to travel alone with me, unchaperoned. To her chagrin, Spits Teeth doesn't care and Fish Basket doesn't attempt to stop us. I wonder what's wrong with this man, to let his daughter travel unchaperoned.

The next day, we set off into the woods. She tells me that she's going to show me where the enemy lives. She points out milestones and quizzes me regularly. "Remember this waterfall. Remember this boulder. Remember this pair of giant trees at the edge of this swamp." Five days later, we climb a tree and spy out over a valley below. She shows me a squirrel's view of Bobcat Mask's village. I'm amazed to see how similar it is to the layout of our own village. We watch tiny specks of people move around in the distant village. Again, she tests me. "What do you see?"

Before we climb down, Ferocious Wind tells me that there is another trail between the villages. We have taken the eastern trail. A western trail runs parallel to it and a mile separates the two. She tells me that we'll return home by the other path. Another trail leads north into the wild woods and mountains. On the way home, she frequently turns me around and tells me to look at the path from the opposite direction.

Halfway back to our village, we are surprised to hear voices in the distance. We look at each other with wide eyes. Ferocious Wind quietly says, "We need to get off the trail." We quickly conceal our travel gear in overgrown bushes. A river runs a short distance from the path. Erosion under the bank, beside the trail, has left a narrow space that can hide us. "Get in," she says. I climb in and lie down. There's barely enough room from head to feet. She climbs in and lies on top of me. I can see her wild eyes from two inches away. "Don't move until I tell you to move. We could be here a very long time." She rests her cheek on my shoulder and relaxes her body.

Despite the dangerous situation, I am completely aware that a half-naked woman with wild eyes is pressed against me. I can feel her breath on my neck. Her breasts are pressed tightly against my chest. I'm sweating worse than I do when we train all day. I feel my heart thumping in my chest and blood races through my body like a raging river in the springtime. It's not the time and it's not the place for it, but romantic thoughts flood my brain. Despite my embarrassing predicament, she remains silent and motionless.

The voices get closer. They stop in the clearing above us and we can hear their conversation. We can tell that it is Bobcat Mask and his son. Their scouts have been spying on our village. They're planning an attack, just days from now. They linger over a leisurely lunch. I'm supposed to relax my body, but I'm as rigid as a tree trunk.

Finally, Bobcat Mask sends the rest of the party on ahead. He climbs over the bank and wanders down to the river. He removes his mask and we can see him eating, though he's facing away from us. He squats and dips his hands into the water and splashes it into his face. Then he stands and warily turns. Whatever has caught his attention doesn't lead his line of sight to our hiding place. Looking at his face is shocking. I'll never forget the sight of the tattoo that mars his skin. He places the mask back on his face, fills his gourd with water and climbs back up to the trail.

We remain glued to each other long after the man has gone. It feels like it has been hours since he left the river. Finally, Ferocious Wind begins to move. She lifts her head from my shoulder. There's a sweet smile on her lips and a rare look of kindness in her eyes. She presses her lips against mine and says, "Tends Hearth is right. We shouldn't be left alone together." Then she slides off me and assumes her usual, ready-to-pounce pose. As I wiggle my way out, I'm thinking of the look in her eyes. It's the first time I've ever seen her with eyes that didn't look crazed. I wonder if I'll ever see that look again. Wondering becomes longing.

We retrieve our pack baskets and Ferocious Wind leads me by the hand into the river. Instead of following the trail, we follow the river for a couple of hours. Our eyes diligently monitor the trail that runs parallel to the river.

At the end of the day, we break for the night. We make a safe, fireless camp a hundred feet from the creek and the trail, beneath some heavy, drooping pine boughs. It's pitch black and we can't see each other, even from a few feet away. Under cover of darkness, I quietly say, "I like you."

She answers, "I can tell."

Then we discuss what we heard and saw. A planned attack.

Seven days from now. We must hasten back and warn the village.

I tell Ferocious Wind that I have met Bobcat Mask and his son before. They were part of the raiding party that rescued me on the banks of the river near the vast ocean. I suggest there must be some kind of an explanation for his face.

Ferocious Wind agrees. "Yes, there must be a reason." Her voice trails off. I wonder if she knows the story. I'm happy not to hear it tonight. It must be a horrible story.

I want to kiss her again. It's dark and she is near, but I'm not sure exactly where. Instead, I wish her a good night and close my eyes. I picture her face just after we kissed. Then that sight of Bobcat Mask's face comes to mind and I shudder. I clasp my hands together over my chest and think of the view from the top of Skellig Michael. I imagine the cool sea breeze at the top of the mountain and the tranquil blue sky and placid ocean, a beautiful sight regardless of which direction you're looking. Picturing it calms me down and I fall into a satisfying sleep.

Ferocious Wind shakes me awake as a hint of dawn begins to light the sky. We make our way to the trail and quicken our pace. We walk with bows in hand, arrows notched. She tells me that we're passing through an area in which game is plentiful. She tells me it might be good if we return home with at least something to show for our hunting trip, and then she winks at me.

The first deer we see is too far away. We spend another night in the woods and the next day we see a second deer. It's a big buck. We both let our arrows fly and the deer drops to the ground immediately. When we get to him, we find that our arrows have crossed, within the heart of the deer. He's so big that both of our baskets are filled to the point of flowing over, and I have his hide draped over my shoulders. Ferocious Wind carries his antlers.

We make it home just as the sun is setting. Something horrible has happened while we were away. Fish Basket wails beneath her blankets, and Black Rat Snake explains. "The women left the longhouse for a few minutes to get some water. Smoky Shrew was tied to the cradleboard. A raccoon got into the longhouse. In less than a minute, it ripped the face off of the baby. It was a horrible sight."

Strips of raccoon meat hang from a rack above the fire. Tends Hearth stands holding the black and white fur in one hand, her other hand on her hip. "More bad luck," she says, with ominous spacing between her words. I'm not sure what she's suggesting, but I want to make the point that I was miles away at the time.

The village council hastily gathers for a meeting. Dancing Bear calls upon the Great Spirit for guidance and protection. Hole in the Roof asks Ferocious Wind to tell the story of our encounter with Bobcat Mask. Then she asks me if I have anything to add. When I describe Bobcat Mask's face beneath his mask, members of the council grumble and look at each other with expressions of surprise. Hole in the Roof asks Spits Teeth what he would advise. "Would it be better to meet the enemy along the trail? Would it be possible to surprise them with an ambush? I'd like the war council to meet at first light, and then we'll all meet together again at mid-day tomorrow."

Chapter 8

The next morning, Tends Hearth demands that I take her to collect mushrooms in the woods across from the lake. She also wants to see the exact location where her brother died. It is rare for Tends Hearth to spend time outdoors, let alone outside the protective palisade walls that surround the village. It is also rare for her to want to spend time with me. Perhaps making me feel guilty is another reason that she insists I accompany her.

Ferocious Wind asks if she can go as well. Tends Hearth protests feebly, failing to find a reason why Ferocious Wind shouldn't join us. We climb into a canoe and begin our trip across the lake.

Every single day, I think about Fragrant's death. Often many times each day. The horror of the tortured expression on his face hasn't faded. The healers assure me that it isn't my fault, and Ferocious Wind agrees. Tends Hearth doesn't say it in so many words, but I know she blames me.

As Ferocious Wind and I paddle, Tends Hearth rides idly in the canoe rather than having to paddle, and she talks non-stop. She spends a minute or two talking about mushrooms, and sweetly asks if we can help her collect them.

Without a transition, she goes from talking about mushrooms to speaking of the river. Her words pack a punch. Sadly, she says, "Mother hasn't stopped crying since *he* died. Every night she cries herself to sleep." Tends Hearth pauses, allowing her words to sink in. Then she adds, "We all do, really. He took such good care of us. Whatever we needed; he would always do it cheerfully." She clears her throat and sniffles. "Of course we were the closest, Fragrant and me. He was in charge of bringing in all of the firewood. I am in charge of keeping the fire in our compartment, and I do most of the cooking."

Tends Hearth makes the cooking sound like a chore. The truth is that it is her favorite thing to do, and she doesn't do too much else. I try to recall what else she does. The only thoughts that come to mind are talking, judging, complaining, and gossiping.

She starts telling Fragrant's life story, with as much detail as possible. Ferocious Wind starts paddling a little faster in the front of the canoe. I match her pace. With each passing paragraph of Tends Hearth's soliloquy, we increase our pace. It isn't long before the canoe violently hits the shore. Tends Hearth is sent flying, crashing into Ferocious Wind, who had braced herself for the impact of the canoe as it approaches the shore.

We spend a couple of hours in the woods. Tends Hearth tells us exactly what kind of mushrooms she is looking for. She advises, "I like the round ones with the dome-shaped tops, the small thumb-sized ones, and the flat-topped ones, but not the brightly colored ones. While we are in the woods, she keeps herself company by vocalizing everything she knows about mushrooms, which is quite a bit. It doesn't take long for us to get beyond earshot. We scurry to fill our baskets with mushrooms and then we hear a screech.

When we get to Tends Hearth, she is on the lowest branch of a pine tree. I spread my arms and ask, "What's wrong?" She points to a snake on some leaves below. Somehow her scream does not scare the snake much.

Ferocious Wind laughs, sending her flint knife flying through the air, pinning the head of the eighteen-inch garter snake to the ground. Amused, she looks back at Tends Hearth perched in the tree and says, "That will be tasty in your mushroom stew."

Tends Hearth climbs back to the ground, picks up her half-full basket of mushrooms and returns to the canoe. Ferocious Wind and I glance at each other, shrug, and bring our mushrooms back to the canoe as well. We climb in and paddle a short distance along the shoreline to the path where Fragrant and I entered the meadow. We glumly traipse up the trail, following in Fragrant's final footsteps. It is slow going. Tends Hearth stops to pick wildflowers along the way.

When we get to the river, Tends Hearth asks me to show her the exact spot. She sits down by the river and dangles her toes in the water. Then she looks up at us and asks, "Can you leave me alone to grieve? I don't think I can concentrate on remembering my brother with you talking to me."

Ferocious Wind shrugs, turns, and motions for me to follow her. We explore the riverside downstream all the way to where it empties into the lake. We had hoped to find the remains of the furs Fragrant had worn that cold winter's day. Nothing. We conclude that he must have been pulled all the way down to the lake, and his bones must be somewhere on the bottom.

During the day, clouds have gathered together. What started as a pleasant, mostly sunny day has turned overcast. The clouds have darkened. We hear a rumble of thunder and we rush back to where we left Tends Hearth. Finally, in the distance, we see her stand up and look to the sky. She opens her mouth in shock. In the flash of a moment, we see a lightning strike head toward her. Tends Hearth raises her arm high, as if that can protect her. We smell it before it hits her. It strikes a tree at the side of the river, then jumps from the lowest branch to her outstretched hand—a side strike. Tends Hearth screams, and then she collapses. We race to her side.

Tends Hearth's body writhes on the ground. She moans loudly. She is not conscious, yet she is expressing the torture of indescribable pain. I gently shake her shoulder. After a moment, she opens her eyes. Her face is twisted in pain. She looks into my eyes. If she could voice her thoughts, I am sure that she would beg me to help her stop her suffering. Ferocious Wind and I guide her to her feet. With hunched shoulders, she stands, sobbing, holding her hand out, palm facing toward the sky. At the center of her hand is a crispy, burned, brown wound. We stand there in the light rain. Tends Hearth's favorite doeskin dress hangs from her body in charred strips.

Ferocious Wind and I quickly discuss what we should do. If there is going to be more lightning, the last place we should be is on the lake in the canoe, yet we are compelled to get Tends Hearth to the healers' home. We convince ourselves that the weather is quickly improving and decide to paddle back. Tends Hearth whimpers, whines, and sobs all the way back. We paddle even faster than we did on our outbound trip.

When we get out of the canoe, we discover that Tends Hearth cannot put weight on her right foot. The rain has stopped and we take a moment to look at her foot. At the bottom of her moccasin, there is a hole the size of a thumbprint, surrounded by burn marks, and there is an ugly black wound on the bottom of her foot where the lightning left her body. Tends Hearth stretches one arm over Ferocious Wind's shoulders, and she stretches her other arm over my shoulders. We shuttle Tends Hearth along as quickly as we can.

Three Fingers and Gathers Seeds jump to help us through their doorway. They help Tends Hearth up to the bed table that I had used when I was in their care. Three Fingers hums reassuringly between questions he directs at Tends Hearth, calling her *pretty girl* instead of using her name. They can't make much sense of her words, except for fragments, like, "It hurts," and "I'm scared," and "help me!"

Three Fingers eventually calms her down with his soothing voice and healing touch. Ever so gently, he touches her skin in various places, "Does this hurt? How about this? Can you feel my touch, pretty girl?"

Gathers Seeds darts back and forth between the table and his collection of medicinal treatments, shaking his head, and tsking from the corner of his mouth at the unusual nature of the wounds.

Three Fingers rolls her over so he can examine her back. He gasps. What he sees takes his breath away. Gathers Seeds's forehead wrinkles, and he triple tsks in rapid succession. I lean toward the table to get a closer look and gulp at the sight. An array of exploded blood vessels has left an enormous pattern on her back, starting with a tree trunk at the small of her back, radiating up to a beautiful spread of branches over her shoulder blades. "The tree of life," I marvel.

Three Fingers gushes, "I've only seen something like this once before, but it wasn't nearly as beautiful as this." Gathers Seeds gently caresses a slippery salve over every inch of Tends Hearth's skin and bandages the wound on her hand with corn silk and dried moss. Half an hour with Three Fingers and Gathers Seeds makes her feel much better. Ferocious Wind and I help her back through the doorway. Three Fingers and Gathers Seeds follow us.

When we reach Tends Hearth's compartment in the longhouse, Three Fingers greets Tends Hearth's mother pleasantly. "Your little girl is very lucky, Loon Feather."

Tends Hearth snaps angrily, her good hand on her hip, "Lucky? I got struck by lightning, and you're calling me lucky?" She is clearly indignant. She turns to look at me, points a finger, and says, "Nothing good ever happens when you are around." She turns to her mother and begs in a childish whimper, "Please help me."

Loon Feather helps her daughter get settled on her bunk on a soft blanket, then she thanks everyone for helping her daughter. She walks Three Fingers and Gathers Seeds halfway home, beyond earshot of Tends Hearth. Gathers Seed assures Loon Feather that

Tends Hearth will recover. Three Fingers agrees but warns that there will be lasting effects. They promise to stop by twice a day to check on their patient before reminding Loon Feather how lucky her daughter is to survive the lightning strike. Three Fingers adds that Ferocious Wind and I have done an excellent job taking care of her and getting her home quickly.

Ferocious Wind and I quietly return to the edge of the lake to take care of the canoe. Tends Hearth's words repeat in my head over and over: "Nothing good ever happens when you are around." Rationally, I know that the lightning strike is not my fault. It also isn't my fault that Fragrant was washed away by the icy river. Yet I feel guilty—in the depths of my soul. Finally, I look at Ferocious Wind and ask, "Did you hear what she said? Nothing good ever happens when you are around!"

Ferocious Wind's nostrils flare, and she shakes her head. "She should feel lucky you are here." Though it is just us by the side of the lake, Ferocious Wind quietly adds, "I can tell you one thing. She'll never leave that longhouse again!" We laugh briefly, then Ferocious Wind says, "If you ask me, it's just as well."

I appreciate her reassurance, but it weighs heavily on my mind anyhow. First Fern. Then Fragrant. Now, Tends Hearth has been struck by lightning. Tends Hearth is right. I am a part of each of these tragedies.

Chapter 9

The next morning, Ferocious Wind announces a competition. It will feature three elements. First, we will race through the rafters of the longhouse, from one end to the other, two hundred feet. Then we will run around the lake. Lastly, we will swim across it and back. Whoever finishes first is the winner. If I beat her, then my training is complete. If she wins, my training must continue.

My biceps have doubled in size since we began training, but my body is heavier than hers. Even so, I make it out of the longhouse just a little ahead of her. On the race around the lake, I open up a bigger lead. I try to move fast while leaving some energy for the long swim to follow. As I'm running, it crosses my mind that I might prefer to lose. I could use a day or two of rest, but I will miss spending these summer days with Ferocious Wind.

The cool water feels good as I splash into it and dive toward the opposite side. As I tear through the water, I feel my legs tire first, leaving much of the work to my arms. Halfway across, I can feel my body slowing and my momentum diminishing. My alternating arms maintain a slow crawl across the surface of the lake and I'm winded by the time I reach the opposite shore. I turn around and see Ferocious Wind has made it three-quarters of the way across the lake. Despite my fatigue, I run back into the water. I wonder if Ferocious Wind is experiencing fatigue also, or whether she has done a better job of pacing herself.

Halfway back, I can hear her. Despite not wanting our training to end, I realize that I'd rather win. I focus all my thoughts on swimming, commanding my legs to kick harder and my arms to swing faster. I'm panting as I swim and each movement hurts. I've seen her swim many times, and her body always seems to glide effortlessly through the water.

During our final approach toward the shore, she has come even with me. Then she speeds up, and I know it is hopeless. I don't have more to give, whereas she has saved some energy for a final push. I can see her watching me as I climb up the bank. My chest is heaving from the exertion. I place my hands on my knees, bend at my waist, and look into her eyes. She won the race but not by much, and she seems exhausted too.

After a couple of minutes, I feel my breath returning, but my heart still races. I'm still looking into her face, and I feel pulled toward her. Finally she takes a couple of steps toward me, as if she feels the tug as I do. I stand up straight in front of her as she approaches.

She says, "You almost beat me."

I nod tentatively.

"They told me I couldn't do it, but look at you now. I have done what they said was impossible." Her eyes scan my body slowly, head to toe, then back again. "You look like a warrior to me."

She tells me to bend my arms at my elbows and flex. She grips my bicep and tells me that I'm powerful. She also praises my weapons skills saying that they have become deadly, almost as good as her own. She smiles, seemingly amused, nods her head, and murmurs approval. She tells me to grip my hands in front of me and flex my chest muscles. Her praise makes me feel jubilant and her touch reverberates throughout my body.

Her poking and prodding becomes a caress. Ever so slightly, I move toward her. In my mind, I'm sweeping her into my arms.

She sidesteps my advance and walks around me. She squeezes

the back of my arms, caresses my shoulders, and her fingertips gently glide down my back. A moment later, I feel her hands gripping my shins. I flex my legs and she moves her hands to my thighs. It's all I can do to stand still when she grabs my posterior. I hold my breath and pray that I can maintain my composure. Finally, she returns to stand in front of me.

Her fingers touch my chest and she gently tugs at a couple of hairs that have recently sprouted there. I tip my head down, close my eyes, and kiss her. I wrap my arms around her. She kisses me back for a couple minutes, then I feel her dancing fingers at my side, tickling me, and she wriggles away from my embrace.

She asks me to lie on my back in the grass, and I become excited about what might happen next. Then she tells me that she has a surprise for me. I think of the things that Fragrant told me about what men and women do together. If Ferocious Wind has any of those things in mind, I'm not sure that I will be able to stop myself.

I watch as she hurries to her pack basket and retrieves some porcupine quills and a covered pot. She sets the pot at my side and sits on my belly. Her knees are buried in my armpits and her feet press into my hips. She raises and lowers her eyebrows a couple of times and says, "This is going to hurt." The way she says it makes it sound like I should enjoy it rather than feel pain.

She holds the barbed end of a quill over my chest and begins stabbing it into my skin, over and over, dozens of times. I am determined not to make a sound about the pain. I don't know why she's doing this, but given my training at Skellig Michael, unquestioning obedience is part of my nature. I don't know what I find more unsettling, the fact that she's stabbing me in the chest or the fact that she's practically sitting on my breechcloth.

Then she reaches for the pot, scoops out some charcoal dust and grinds it into my skin. She tells me to close my eyes, and I feel her breath on my chest as she blows the excess dust away. My eyes are still closed and I jump when she starts stabbing me with the quill again. I should have figured it out sooner, but that's when I realize that she's making a tattoo over my heart. I wonder why she is doing this, and I try to guess at what the design will look like when she's done.

It feels like she's been sitting on me for hours when she finally stands up, looks down at me and says, "Now it's my turn." She must be reading the look of horror on my face. "It's easy." Then she lies down next to me and tells me to get up and get to work.

I look down at the mess of black lines on my chest and try to make out the design. I take a deep breath and tell myself that I can do this. "First, can you draw the design in the dirt with a stick, so I know what it should look like?"

She draws two arrows, complete with feathers on one end and arrowheads on the other, and the arrows cross each other a short distance from the pointy ends. Then she points to her breast and tells me where to start and where to end. I'm nervous to touch her, but when I finally do, she laughs, like I'm tickling her. I'm also reticent about the meaning of the matching symbols. I'm afraid of hurting her, although she seems to delight in experiencing pain. As I make the first prick with the quill, she tells me to make sure that I dig deep enough, or the color won't take. By the time I get to the end of the first arrow, I get up the courage to ask her about the significance of our matching tattoos. Her answer is that we are celebrating the end of our training, and the arrows are to remind us of the deer we killed together. I can't help but think there is more to it than that.

After the tattoos are done, we stretch out, side by side on the grass, looking up into the sky. We talk about the time we've spent on our relentless training schedule. We relive the previous day's traumatic lightning strike that Tends Hearth miraculously survived. Then Ferocious Wind starts to talk about the various ways we might be called upon to fight our enemy. I reach my arm toward her and take her hand in mine. She's excited about striking the enemy, the sooner the better. I feel my belly churn. I'd rather use my strength in other pursuits. An image comes to mind of Lector Beccán kneeling, his tonsured head tipped forward, and his hands folded in prayer. It's hard to be a warrior when you've spent a lifetime among pacifists. I think of the monks' commitment to living a life of poverty, chastity, and obedience. I'm still holding Ferocious Wind's hand and I'm thinking about her sitting on me while she tattooed me. I wonder what Lector Beccán would think if he knew what I am imagining. I glance sideways at the woman next to me, and I think that just because I was raised by monks doesn't mean I have to follow their vows. I should be able to get married if I want to. I wonder how I will get married in the wilds of whatever land I'm in. Then I realize that I've stopped listening to Ferocious Wind. Finally, she has grown quiet and suggests that we go swimming. I think I'd rather just stay here and see what happens. I cast my thoughts aside and follow her.

When we get to the lake, I realize that she has a different sort of swim in mind. As a warrior woman, she wears the breechcloth of a man. As the breechcloth hits the ground, I see her fully naked form. I can't take my eyes off her. She walks backward into the lake and motions for me to join her. She raises an eyebrow and I hurry toward her. "I'd better leave mine on, or we'll both be sorry," I tell her. We kiss again, then I ask, "Is this allowed? Since I was adopted, does that make me your brother?"

She says, "No." Then she turns and dives into the water. I'm left to wonder whether she just told me no, it isn't allowed, or no, I'm not her brother.

After our swim, we join the men in the woods and spend the afternoon chopping wood. I find it comforting doing steady, repetitive work. It feels good to be working on something that will help people survive during the winter. I can't shake the sight of Ferocious Wind dropping her breechcloth. Is it proper to be this obsessed? Maybe it is better if we don't spend time alone together.

When we get back to the longhouse, everyone is ready for dinner. Tends Hearth turns toward me and Ferocious Wind and says, "I saw you straddling Conchobar down by the river when I went to use the latrine. Only yesterday, I was struck by lightning. You should be taking care of me instead of doing—" she pauses and increases her volume, "that." Then she notices the tattoos on our chests. She points, shakes her finger and says, "And what is this? Matching tattoos?"

Tends Hearth's face is twisted in what I figure must be disgust. I turn to look at Ferocious Wind just as she turns to face me.

Her sister is instantly forgotten as I gaze into Ferocious Wind's eyes. I can't help but wish I was back at the river with her.

Chapter 10

The next night, the healers join us for dinner. Curiously, I ask, "Why do we hate Bobcat Mask and his people?" The immediate response is shocked silence. It would seem that such questions are rarely asked, and if they are, they aren't worded in such a fashion.

After a pause, Spits Teeth asks Three Fingers to tell his story. Three Fingers has heard the story many times.

He hesitates, and I wonder if he'd rather be telling a different story from the one that he is preparing to tell. He sets his food down so he can concentrate on telling the story the way Spits Teeth would want it told. "Thirty-two years ago, Spits Teeth was captured. He was just a 9-year-old boy. As a child, he was known as Whittler. On a dare, a very brave enemy entered Whittler's village during the light of day, unnoticed. Whittler was sitting on a log beside a fire, enjoying his favorite activity, whittling twigs, so you can see how he got his name. The warrior snuck up on the boy, covered Whittler's mouth with his hand, and plucked him from his seat beside the fire. The boy wiggled, squirmed, and convulsed, attempting to break away. He was unsuccessful. A mile away, his captor put him on the ground, and Whittler took off running. It didn't take the grown man long to recapture the boy."

Three Fingers stands up, tilts his head and continues. "Try to imagine: What did Whittler think? How did he feel? How did he behave? What did his captor say? What did the captor do to Whittler along the way?" Three Fingers looked from me to Ferocious Wind, then back to me again as he continued. "Sometimes he would kick the boy to make him move faster. He berated Whittler. He told Whittler all the terrible, horrible things that would happen to him when they arrived at their village."

Spits Teeth and Three Fingers's eyes meet, then Three Fingers looks back toward the rest of us. "Whittler had seen how captives were treated in his own village. He knew being captured was possibly worse than being killed. Would he be tortured and then killed? Would he die bravely and honor his family and his people? Would he act like a child, and beg, scream, and cry? Would he be adopted by a family that had lost a child? Would he become a slave? Whittler puffed out his chest, set his jaw firmly, and resolved to be silent no matter what the outcome." I glance at Spits Teeth and notice that he has puffed out his chest and set his jaw firmly, just as Three Fingers described in the story.

I look back at the healer and he continues. "Whittler's captors were busy making final preparations for the long winter to come. He wasn't an impressive catch, as captives go, just a scrawny boy, a long way from becoming a man. He endured his tormenters' beatings bravely, defiantly, and silently. Mercifully, they quickly lost interest. If he had behaved like a screaming, crying child, they might have enjoyed that more. If he had fought them, they might have been more entertained."

Three Fingers stretches his arms to indicate the passing of time within his story. "For the next six years, Whittler remained a captive servant, forced to sleep on the ground at the foot of the bed belonging to Hump Nose, the war chief of the village. Each night they tied him up. His arms were tied together then tied to the post at the head of the bunk. His ankles were tied together and tied to the foot of the bed. For six long years, he fought to remember everything about his parents, his siblings, his longhouse, and their village. He strived to memorize every detail from home by repetition. He also memorized everything he could about his captors, organizing details in his brain for future use."

The healer walks around the fire as he speaks and sits between Ferocious Wind and me. "The chief's oldest child, a boy about Whittler's age, was a child who could do no wrong. He enjoyed the favor of everyone in the village, especially his father, Hump Nose. He was a boy called Thin Cheeks. Every day, Whittler tended to all the menial tasks Hump Nose's family ordered him to perform. More than any other task, Whittler had to chop wood. You can see his strong arms and chest muscles still, from having chopped all that wood, way back then." Three Fingers stretches his arm in the direction of Spits Teeth, reminding us that the story of Whittler is also the story of Spits Teeth. "Nobody in their family ever had to chop firewood. He did such a good job providing for Hump Nose's family, that Hump Nose would often barter him to other families for their use."

Three Fingers pauses for half a minute, signaling a change in the story he is telling. "It was a proud time for Hump Nose's family. Thin Cheeks was 15-years-old. Hump Nose was preparing for his son's rite of passage. For weeks, it seemed, that was all that they could talk about or think about. Whittler, who was also 15-years-old, heard every detail, knowing that if he were in his own village, he would also be preparing for manhood. Of course, nobody thought that Whittler too might experience a transformation."

Everyone around the fire is hanging on every word in the story. Three Fingers begins speaking faster. "One afternoon, Thin Cheeks set off on his journey. The next day, while chopping wood for a friend of Hump Nose, Whittler found a sharp flint knife, which he quickly wrapped in green leaves and awkwardly concealed within his breechcloth. Whittler was sure others would notice, though nobody ever really looked at him, beyond barking an order, or making sure he never escaped. They had gotten so used to watching over Whittler, they did it automatically, while seeing right through him. The day Whittler found the knife he had the good fortune to be able to get it into the longhouse. Hump Nose's wife had her back turned, and Whittler was supposed to be building a fire at the hearth. He managed to quickly conceal the knife beneath some dust on the dirt floor. He hoped it was just where he could reach it later that evening after he was tied up for the night."

I glance at Spits Teeth, whose chin sits high in the air while Three Fingers pauses briefly to let the audience catch up to his story. "It was the second night of Thin Cheeks's vigil. Whittler had heard every detail in the plan. He knew exactly where the boy would be. Thin Cheeks would become a powerful man, perhaps a chief, like his father. Whittler knew he would remain an invisible servant, tied to the bed of the chief for the rest of his life, unless he found a way to escape."

Three Fingers whispers, "He waited until everyone was fast asleep. He was all too familiar with every sound Hump Nose made in bed. When the whole family was snoring, Whittler began sawing the ropes that bound his hands, barely moving the twisted cordage against the sharp flint blade. He was sure others could hear the sawing sounds of the fibers breaking free, though he tried to conceal the sound within the rhythm of Hump Nose's snores, one direction when he inhaled, then back when he exhaled. Eventually the bond broke loose. He was glad they were sleeping so soundly, because he was sure his heart was beating loudly enough to be heard, even if the quiet sawing sound of flint on rope wasn't loud enough. When he was free, he scooped up a couple of handfuls of cold charcoal at the edge of the fire. Then he helped himself to Hump Nose's favorite weapons and his best pack basket. Finally, he tiptoed out into the light of a full moon."

Three Fingers glances at Spits Teeth again, who seems to be appreciating Three Finger's version of his story. "It didn't take Whittler long to find Thin Cheeks. During their planning, Hump Nose and Thin Cheeks had described the location perfectly. They didn't even notice the intensity with which Whittler had listened. They didn't see the hatred in his eyes. Whittler thought briefly about the fact that it had been years since anyone had looked directly into his eyes, the way his mother had when he was a child, back in his birth village."

I breathe deeply as Three Fingers pauses again. "Whittler found Thin Cheeks, fast asleep, in a fetal position. It didn't look to Whittler like Thin Cheeks was suffering in the slightest during his three-day ordeal. He had never hoped to imagine what revenge he would unleash in such a moment. It came to him on the spot. Whittler tossed himself onto Thin Cheeks's body. The boy was immobilized by Whittler's weight and surprised by the sudden, unexpected attack. Suddenly awake, Thin Cheeks saw the depth of hatred burning from Whittler's eyes. He saw an evil grin building on the lips of the captive he had long taken for granted. Thin Cheeks recognized he was pinned. Whittler's hand was planted firmly on his forehead, and his strong arm held Thin Cheeks's head firmly planted against the ground. Whittler's weight sat heavily on the middle of Thin Cheeks's stomach. Even in the dead of night, Thin Cheeks saw the knife in Whittler's right hand."

Three Fingers places his hand in the middle of his own forehead for emphasis. "Whittler turned Thin Cheeks's head sideways. He was powerless to resist. Whittler deeply sliced into his cheek. A thick bead of blood jumped to the surface of Thin Cheeks's skin in the wake of the path of the flint blade. The grin on Whittler's face widened as he turned Thin Cheeks's head all the way to the other side. The knife blade repeated the image on the boy's other cheek—an image that no man would want carved onto his face. If their lifetimes hadn't already been linked together through hatred, that connection was consummated in that moment. Whittler tied Thin Cheeks's hands and ankles, just as Whittler had been tied each night for six years. In place of bed posts, Thin Cheeks was tied between two trees. Then Whittler ground the charcoal dust into Thin Cheeks's wounds. After that, Whittler cut the string at the band of his breechcloth, stuffed the dirty garment into Thin Cheeks's mouth, and tied the gag firmly in place around his head. Then he took Thin Cheeks's breechcloth for his own, leaving his enemy naked in the night. Whittler stood and watched Thin Cheeks's steely composure weaken as a grimace crossed his bloody face, an expression of the pain, anger, and shame he felt. Whittler felt victorious and momentarily avenged as he urinated on his former captor's face. Then Whittler was gone."

Three Fingers stands again, and stretches his arms wide, preparing to conclude his story. "Whittler couldn't remember having ever felt better than he did at that moment. After six years of slavery, Whittler felt completely free. He had thought about it every night as he fell asleep, so he would remember the way they had come, six years earlier. He traveled due south, and he envisioned a hero's homecoming. As he traveled through the night, Whittler's life purpose came into his mind. He imagined Hump Nose discovering his escape. He smiled at the thought of Hump Nose finding that his favorite weapons were missing. The evil grin returned to Whittler's face as he fantasized Hump Nose discovering his favorite child's humiliation during his rite of passage. Whittler chuckled to think that he wished for Thin Cheeks to survive, so he would be forced to tell Whittler's story to his people. Having accomplished escape, his new mission was to obliterate their village. If he couldn't do that, he would kill as many as he could before they could kill him."

I wonder whether Three Fingers is enjoying telling Spits Teeth's story as he puts his hands on his hips and continues. "Early one morning, the following summer a party of warriors attacked Hump Nose's village. Whittler's insider knowledge helped the war party's success. In less than an hour, half of its population had been killed, and the other half escaped on foot. Whittler had rejoiced at slaying Hump Nose with the man's own tomahawk, in the first moments of the battle. Thin Cheeks awakened in time to mount a defense, his war club connecting with Whittler's mouth, which gave Thin Cheeks the few minutes he needed to escape. Whittler spit his front teeth out from between his bloodied lips, then Whittler killed the rest of the members of Hump Nose's family. Finally, the surviving members of Hump Nose's war council were able to mount enough of a counter-attack to encourage the retreat of Whittler's war party. Nobody could remember a more successful raid. The men traveled swiftly south, stopping occasionally for a drink of water, and some self-congratulatory retelling of the battle scene, practicing for the stories they'd tell upon their return home. At their first rest stop, Whittler's uncle noticed Whittler's torn lips and missing teeth. Whittler told his uncle that he spit them on the dead body of his captor. He told his uncle he would never repeat the name of his captor, and he would never forget the ugly face of that man either."

During another brief pause, I say my thoughts out loud. "So that's how Spits Teeth got his name."

Three Fingers nods. "Yes, Whittler's uncle proclaimed, 'from now on you will be known as Spits Teeth. The boy known as Whittler no longer exists.' And that is how our war chief became He Who Spits Teeth."

Ferocious Wind asks about Thin Cheeks.

Three Fingers says, "I forgot to tell you that part. To cover his disfigured cheeks, Thin Cheeks wears a mask, fashioned from the head of a bobcat. Now he is known as Bobcat Mask. As Spits Teeth discovered the night of our attack, Thin Cheeks, now Bobcat Mask, even sleeps in the mask, which is strapped so tightly to his head, it wouldn't matter how many times he flipped and flopped in his sleep at night. Make no mistake about it, Bobcat Mask and Spits Teeth have the same purpose: total annihilation of the village of the other."

Spits Teeth stands proudly, crosses his arms over his chest and nods. In a rare, reflective tone, he observes, "I'm not getting any younger. It is time to put an end to Bobcat Mask. If something happens to me, it is up to you," he concludes, swiping his chin up into the air in the direction of Black Rat Snake.

After the healers leave, I climb to my bunk. Before long people are snoring all around me. Spits Teeth is coupling with Loon Feather and grunting loudly. I press my fingers in my ears and wonder whether six years of slavery would have affected me the same as it did Spits Teeth. He has made it clear that he expects his family to advance his mission beyond his own lifetime, should he fail to complete it himself. I never would have thought I could feel empathy for this man, yet the way he treats his wives, I resolve to dispel notions of sympathy for Spits Teeth.

When the longhouse becomes completely quiet, and everyone is asleep, I feel my eyelids growing heavy. I hope I don't have that horrible nightmare again tonight.

Chapter 11

The council spends all day discussing strategy. Despite Spits Teeth's dream of destroying Bobcat Mask's village, protecting our own village is the council's highest priority. Our most experienced warriors are assigned to defense. Spits Teeth argues with Hole in the Roof. He wants to send twenty men to attack their village, which will be vulnerable. She sits motionless and expressionless, hands folded in her lap, staring forward at nothing in particular, like a blind woman.

Spits Teeth paces in front of her, frustrated, arms swinging, emphasizing our advantage and opportunity. Finally, he lowers his request to a dozen eager young warriors. Hole in the Roof answers simply. "No."

Spits Teeth stomps his feet, sputters, and begs. Having witnessed the way Spits Teeth treats his wives and ignores his daughter, I'm amazed that an old woman who barely acknowledges his presence can hold such power over him. Spits Teeth repeats his arguments and the pitch of his voice raises in desperation as his pleas continue unheeded. Then he squats immediately in front of Hole in the Roof, inches from her face, and peers directly into her eyes and lowers his requisition. "I shall lead a party of eight warriors into the enemy's village."

Hole in the Roof raises her voice. I've never heard her speak more than a couple of words. She proclaims, "*Our* war chief shall remain in *our* village. A party of eight warriors can be sent to attack the enemy if it pleases the council. Let us vote." Then she sends Spits Teeth away.

I find it unsettling to see the powerful man dismissed by an elderly woman. She speaks for another couple of minutes, stands, and presides over the voting. The plan is nearly unanimously approved. Dancing Bear stands and offers prayers and predictions. I glance at Three Fingers and catch him sharing a knowing look with Gathers Seeds. In the past, I've noticed their doubting expressions whenever Dancing Bear speaks. Today, it's even more apparent. The two very different looking faces mirror a similar cringe. My stomach churns with foreboding and the realization that something terrible is going to happen. When powerful, equally matched enemies meet, how is tragedy to be avoided? I'm grateful that the wisdom of Hole in the Roof has prevailed. And then I learn that I'm one of the eight that will attack Bobcat Mask's village.

After the council adjourns, the war council convenes. One by one, Spits Teeth names off the warriors that will mount our offense. Black Rat Snake is named first, and he is named as the leader of the raid. Ferocious Wind and Earth Shakes are added to the roster. Spits Teeth asks Black Rat Snake who else he'd like to take with him, and Black Rat Snake pans the assembled warriors, choosing four men our age. Then he looks at me, shrugs, and says my name. He makes a few bold remarks. "It will be a glorious victory." If Black Rat Snake is right, I will have to slay innocent enemies in their homes. If he's wrong, our village will mourn the loss of its strongest young warriors. Black Rat Snake brags, "What could possibly go wrong?" I shudder as the words hang around me. The crowd disperses until I'm standing alone, fearing victory and defeat.

I seek Three Fingers's counsel. He listens to me while I voice my dilemma, nodding sympathetically. He asks a couple of questions, then he offers advice. "I wish that we didn't have to battle our enemies. It would make me happy if we could find a way to befriend them. Unfortunately, we are in a time where we must deal with the situation as it is. You must fight as if your life depends on it. You must find a way to rationalize brutality. Fight to save yourself. Imagine what they'll do to Ferocious Wind if they capture her. Fight to save yourself. Fight as if you are defending your future unborn children. Fight so that one day you can sit among the children of your children. Imagine the enemy with a knife at *my* throat. You must act as if *our* lives depend on it. Don't think of the enemy as humans. I'm sorry, there's no other way."

I nod, sadly acknowledging that Three Fingers's advice is exactly what I need to hear. Then I look back into Three Fingers's eyes and ask, "What about Dancing Bear's prediction of a glorious victory?"

Three Fingers frowns. "Dancing Bear is our sachem, but there's nothing to him. He says what is required. The Great Spirit does not live within his soul. He is an empty pot. Fortunately, I think the Great Spirit dances in the soul of Hole in the Roof. I believe we will be victorious, but victory always comes at a cost during times of war." Three Fingers is quiet for a minute. His words roll through my brain. Then he continues, "A warrior lives to battle. A true warrior can't be happy without the challenge of a battle. Either there is a warrior in your soul or there is not. Soon, you shall know. That is all." Three Fingers drapes his arm over my shoulder and walks me to his doorway.

It has been days since Ferocious Wind and I heard Bobcat Mask speak of their attack. Our village has prepared its defense. Our raiding party has planned its attack. Spits Teeth has instructed our primary plan, and half a dozen contingent plans have been devised. Our objective is to kill as many of the enemy as we can, and we are to burn as much of their property as possible. No captives. No plunder. It is an annihilation campaign. Then we are to retreat along the western path, looking for opportunities to kill any warriors that might be retreating from their attack on our village. It seems like too big a job for a group as small as ours, but I am not the leader. I was raised to be obedient, and so I shall be.

Five days later, our party stands at the foot of the tree where Ferocious Wind and I scouted the enemy village, not so long ago. The members of our party scamper up the large tree, high up into its branches, and I stand on the ground, both hands on the trunk of the tree.

My hands tingle. I feel a strange wave of energy permeate my body. I close my eyes and I feel the passing of time. Instead of two arms I feel as if I have hundreds of arms, or branches instead. I feel a sense of growing, expanding, strengthening and weakening. The seasons roll across me and I see my surroundings change from spring to summer to autumn to winter. The passing of time slows somewhat and I see the enemy's village being built, hardworking people making themselves a home to sustain themselves. Time speeds up as if I'm watching the lives of the dots in the distant village. They live their whole lives in the span of half of a minute. Then it is over. I'm amazed that the tree has shared its memories with me. I'm in awe to have felt what it is like to be a tree. I am glad that the spirit of God lives within a tree and radiates such glory. As I climb up the branches, I feel the sensation of eight people stepping lightly on my arms.

The ancient tree stands witness to our final battle plans. Three Fingers's words play in my mind. I tell myself that the enemy are raccoons disguised as humans. They wish to rip our faces off, like the raccoon that killed poor Smoky Shrew. I won't take unnecessary risks, and I'll be on the lookout for protecting our party if I can.

We sleep fitfully in shifts at the base of the lookout tree. Black Rat Snake wakes us an hour before dawn. He places his hand over the tattoo on my chest and says, "Today you will become a warrior, my brother." Blood thunders through my veins as we tiptoe across the dew laden sedges and enter through the unguarded palisade gates of the enemy's town.

As we planned, we have split into teams of two. I follow Ferocious Wind into the first longhouse on the right. I watch as she flicks her knife across the throat of a man in the first bunk. I feel a wave of nausea as I prepare to slit the throat of the man in a bunk directly across the aisle. His eyes open and look deep into my soul at the moment my blade slices through his neck. I try not to think about anything as my knife slits the throat of the woman that lies beside him. We tiptoe through the compartments of the longhouse, repeating our ghastly offenses upon family after family.

In the last compartment, when I get to the top bunk, I see a young boy with a bow. He's notching an arrow, and his eyes are staring at the back of Ferocious Wind. One by one, she deftly slits the throats of his cousins across the aisle. I reach for the club at my side and swing it with all the power I can muster, smashing the little boy's brain. I try to convince myself it is the same as when we swung the clubs at rotting stumps in the swamp. But it isn't the same. I will never forget the crunching sound of the war club cracking that boy's skull despite the fact that I swiftly killed twenty-five people before I killed him. But there's no time to think about that now.

We scoop burning logs from the fire pits into the beds of the dead bodies, returning through the longhouse the way we came. Then we fly through the doorway just in time to see Black Rat Snake carrying the dead body of his brother.

An archer across the green stretches his bow. Ferocious Wind screams at her brother, telling him to drop to the ground. Instead he runs faster. An arrow flies from the strings of the archer's bow. I run as fast as I can toward Black Rat Snake, as if I could run faster than an arrow can fly. The arrow pierces my brother's skin and passes through his heart. I crash into him before he falls and the impact sends our dead brother flying to the ground. Ferocious Wind throws Earth Shakes over her shoulder as I lift Black Rat Snake. We speed toward the palisade gates and race along our planned escape route. Three of the other four warriors have survived as well. They cover our retreat as the village of our enemies comes fully awake. Fortunately for us, most of their warriors are in our village instead of theirs.

Our months of physical conditioning have paid off. I try to force every thought from my mind. I must move fast down this trail and I must bring my dead brother's body home. I must not think of the dying man's eyes, the wife at his side, the young boy at the dying end of my warclub, or the dozens of innocent people I killed today. I wonder how many people were killed by the other members of our party. Our enemy's village must have a fraction of the population that it had before. Is it worth the price of two dead brothers? I scoff at the notion of a glorious victory. I feel Black Rat Snake's body slide from my sweaty shoulders. I heft his limp body from the dusty path and return to running down the road. Our three surviving comrades are covering our retreat with their bows drawn, yet I push ahead as if we are running for our lives.

After we reach a safe distance from the enemy's village, we take turns carrying the dead bodies. Ferocious Wind leads the way home. We travel as fast as we can, mindful that we will cross paths with the enemy in retreat.

When we reach the spot where Ferocious Wind and I encountered Bobcat Mask at the riverside, we switch from the fast-moving path to travel the riverbed instead. Attacking the retreating enemy had been part of our strategy, but the dead bodies over our shoulders have changed that plan.

As we enter our village, severed limbs, blood, and dead bodies are all around us. There's a victory celebration underway in the center of our village. I feel the weight of a mountain on my shoulders as

I deliver the dead body of the war chief's favorite son to the village green. Ferocious Wind tells the story. She proudly speaks of her warrior brothers who have died in a glorious battle and the many enemies they dispatched.

Tends Hearth stands at her side, looks at her dead brothers, and sobs. "The curse of Conchobar strikes again."

Her father, who never pays attention to Tends Hearth, looks at her and mouths the words. *The curse of Conchobar.*

I open my mouth to defend myself, but decide to stifle my denial, leaving my thoughts unspoken. I saved your daughter. I killed two dozen people. I carried your dead son's body home. This was all your plan, not mine. How is your son's death my fault?

Chapter 12

Ferocious Wind argues vociferously. "Conchobar was nowhere near Black Rat Snake and Earth Shakes when they were killed. He fought valiantly and killed more of the enemy than we usually kill in years of skirmishes, and if it weren't for him, *I* would have an arrow in *me*. Conchobar is a hero. And a warrior."

Tends Hearth screams, "Must I remind everyone, since *that one* arrived here, Fern has been squashed by a tree. Fragrant has drowned in the river. I was struck by lightning, mother lost the baby she was carrying, and Smoky Shrew had her face ripped off. Now, Black Rat Snake and Earth Shakes are gone as well. *That one* shall no longer be known as Conchobar. Instead, he shall be known as Cursed."

Spits Teeth turns, look up at me and says, "My son is gone. He stretched his arm and pointed south. Get your things and go. You *are* cursed. I banish you."

My jaw is clenched. I turn and walk swiftly to the longhouse to gather my meager possessions. Tends Hearth's words hang heavy in my head. It hurts to be blamed. I feel the shame of having destroyed Ferocious Wind's family. It also hurts to be sent away, though I can't blame Spits Teeth. If I were him, I would probably send me away too. Mostly I'm angry. How could I let them convince me to kill innocent people as they slept in their bunks? I should have refused the warrior's path. I would probably still be banished, but at least I wouldn't feel like a murderer.

Ferocious Wind follows me to the longhouse. She adds several things to my basket that she thinks I'll find useful. I am grateful that she followed me and for the gifts she sends me off with. I look around to make sure we are alone, kiss her quickly, thank her, and turn to go. Despite recalling that Spits Teeth ordered me to head south, I head in the opposite direction. Since I have been banished, I no longer feel a duty to obey the man.

It's several hours until dark and I aim to get as far as I can. I wonder if I'll ever escape the shame I feel. I'd like to rationalize that I was a captive. I did what I was told to do. How could I have done otherwise? I could wallow in the notion of being banished, thrown away, discarded. I tuck my unruly hair behind my ears and feel my mood improving. I should think of myself as liberated. I breathe deeply and inhale freedom. I shall have to learn how to survive on my own in this strange land.

I have never felt more homesick. Maybe I'll feel better if I think of a time when I was most happy. My mind travels back in time. It's hard to remember when I began working with the chisel and mallet. Perhaps it was seven years ago. I think of my work with the monks, building steps from the sea to the summit. Crafting each step took about a week. At first the work was hard, yet it was satisfying to see the results materialize before my eyes, each step a perfect, smooth rectangle.

I wasn't the only one that worked on the steps. Some days, as many as five of us would busily tap away at the stone. If I had to carve the steps by myself, it would probably have taken twenty-five years instead of five. The monks from the Abbey weren't talkative, so I was grateful for the company of a large colony of puffins that made their home on Skellig Michael from April to August.

One family of puffins became so comfortable with my presence on the island they seemed to accept me as one of their own. When I needed to take a break, I'd sit and watch the playful birds flap their wings, tumble over each other, roll around, and crash into each other. Their antics perfectly matched their appearance. I loved watching them waddle on their stubby orange feet. Their faces looked so expressive. They had chubby white cheeks, distinctive black triangular marks over their eyes, and oddly shaped, oversized orange striped beaks. Without their black hoods and matching black capes that covered their backs and wings, they wouldn't have been puffins. I had never seen a more pure-white color than the bellies of those puffins.

Each day, one particular puffin would wander over and check on my progress. Sometimes he was joined by his mate, and when their egg hatched, I could look forward to meeting the newest member of their family. It was hard to be in a bad mood when they were around. Compared to the ugly brown falcons that also called the island home, the brilliantly colored beauties seemed all the more spectacular. It's a silly thing, I suppose, to think that what I miss the most are those foolish birds.

The joy of recalling the puffins is short-lived. As my feet move hastily up the trail, my thoughts return to my time in Spits Teeth's village. I know I wasn't meant to live in a longhouse. I wasn't meant to spend all my time in big herds of people. Sleeping in stacks of bunks is way too intimate for my taste. It felt good to be welcomed, at least initially, until the curse caught up with me. I'm glad to have my space despite the sting of ostracism.

Mostly, I miss Ferocious Wind. I can't stop thinking about the wild woman. I ache for her and my chest feels like it will collapse. Yet being around her is unsettling. I can't control my thoughts or desires. Her unpredictable nature scares me. She's the opposite of me in almost every way. I may not be a warrior, but she definitely is. It doesn't make sense and it makes me sick to admit it, but there isn't anything I wouldn't do if she asked me to. Nevertheless, I'm devastated by the memory of sliding my blade across the necks of her enemies. Every time I think of it, which is about every five minutes, my cheeks feel hot and I am angry with myself.

I notice that some of the leaves on the trees are turning from green to various shades of red, orange, brown, and yellow. Where I'm from there are few trees, and I'm not used to seeing the dazzling display that comes with the changing of the season, from summer to autumn. Heavy snowfall isn't common at Skellig Michael either, but from last winter I remember the bitter cold and snow so deep we needed special giant shoes to walk around in it. I know that my adopted family pampered me during my first winter in this new land. This next winter on my own will be a challenge to survive. I shall need lots of wood to burn, and a shelter to protect me. How shall I feed myself? I'm grateful for the time spent training with Ferocious Wind. Physical conditioning and hunting skills will be crucial to surviving the brutal winter to come.

I'm mindful that I must be quick. I have a lot to do, and I want to get as far away from the feuding villages as I can get. But first, I have to get past Bobcat Mask's village, undetected.

Finally, it is too dark to see the trail ahead of me. I turn from the trail into the woods, crashing through the dead branches that cling to tree trunks at ground level until I find cover beneath the sweeping boughs of a hemlock tree.

I hear the distant howl of wolves, and I think of the raccoon that ripped off the baby's face, and I wonder what other evil creatures lurk within this dark forest. I will have to learn to survive among them. I pray for safety, I pray for forgiveness, and then I wait for sleep to find me.

In the morning, a sense of being cold awakens me well before dawn. To pass the time, I sit in the dark, stroking the feathery foliage of the hemlock tree. I feel a tingly sensation in my fingers, and the tips of my fingers glow with a dim light, as if some sort of energy from the massive tree has passed, from it to me. Though my feet are still cold, I feel a warming sensation in my chest. It feels like the tree is stretching its bough and wrapping it around me like a blanket. I feel protected. It reminds me of when Lector Beccán would wrap me up in a warm wool blanket when I was a child.

I shake my head quickly, hoping to clear my mind. Are you going mad? This is just a tree.

Then the words appear in my head, as if someone is speaking to me. You prayed for safety and you prayed for forgiveness. I put my head in my hands and speak aloud. "If only it were that easy."

At midday, I get a sick feeling in my stomach. I don't know what makes me think it's necessary, but I hastily retreat into the thick woods, trying to be quiet and careful not to leave a trail of broken branches like I usually do. Then I lay on the ground. A dozen of the enemy jog up the trail that I had been walking on. I can't explain how I knew to leave the trail and take cover. Could it be divine providence? What else could it be? Whatever the explanation, I'm grateful. I am looking forward to getting as far away from their village as I can.

I must still be tired because I fall asleep on the ground in the middle of the day. It's just as well. I want to make sure the trail is safe to travel. What if the enemy took a break and I walked directly into them? I rub my eyes and try to figure out how long I have been asleep. Perhaps an hour, I suppose. I notice some blueberries growing a short distance away. I'm instantly aware that I'm desperately hungry. I run to the blueberries as if there is some kind of danger that they might flee. I pick the sweet, yet tart berries and pop them in my mouth. They explode between my teeth. I shove them in so fast I almost bite my own fingers. I've had my fill, but I keep eating, not sure when my next meal might come.

I'm surprised by a giant crashing noise that reminds me of the time Fern was squashed by a tree. This crashing noise isn't nearly as powerful, but still concerning. I quickly look in each direction, trying to find the source of the noise. A big black bear lumbers from the depths of the woods in a motion that almost looks like he's rolling. He looks at me. He knows I'm here. I wish I weren't. I haven't seen a bear before. He makes himself comfortable in a patch of blueberries, just as I have done. I decide it would be a good idea to leave this section of the woods to him, and slowly make my way back toward the trail.

The bear stands and I freeze. He slowly moves in my direction, and I melt into the ground. If only I were small enough to disappear beneath the blueberry shrubs. I'm shivering with fear. The massive bear stops fifteen feet from me at a gigantic tree with rough bark. He stretches his body as tall as he can and scratches the tree with his sharp claws. With his back to me, I rise again and back away from the bear, putting as much distance as I can between him and me. Then he turns around and scratches his hindquarters against the tree. He's watching me, but his itches are more important than whatever I'm doing. Finally, I can't see him anymore, but I can still hear him flopping around in the woods. When I'm a safe distance from the bear, I permit myself to covet his warm coat. Winter will be much warmer if I can wrap myself up in the fur of a bear. As if I don't have enough to worry about, now I can't shake the fear of those fierce claws that ripped the bark off the old tree. Yet I wonder if the tree feels pain within the scars left by the bear?

A little farther up the trail, I see a small clearing full of decaying deadfall. I see a stump with clusters of turkey tail mushrooms. It is astonishing how closely the multi-colored fungus fans out, just like the tailfeathers of an old tom turkey. I fill my half-empty pack basket with as many of the mushrooms as I can. Next time I'm hungry, I'll be glad to have them in my possession.

I try to remember the markers that Ferocious Wind showed me when we traveled this path. I feel like I should reach our spying tree anytime now. Everything looks familiar but not distinctive, yet I can feel that it isn't far away. I hate being this close to the enemy's village. If only I can make it to the tree that makes me feel safe.

Chapter 13

There's just enough light to make it safely into the branches of the majestic maple tree that feels like an old friend. To protect the mushrooms in my pack basket from birds, squirrels, and chipmunks I have woven some hemlock branches across the top of the basket. With the basket wedged safely between branches just high enough to be out of sight, I find a comfortable limb nearby. I use a vine that I picked up earlier in the day to tie myself to a branch in case I should roll from the tree in my sleep. It is hard to imagine finding a comfortable place to sleep in a tree, but I have found a perfect pair of branches.

Looking out over the village in the distance makes me feel sad. It is a chilling melancholy, like the deep ocean that seems like it has no bottom. I wish that I could stop thinking about the people I killed in that village. A feeling of shame overcomes my melancholy. The dots that move around the village complex are far less plentiful than when we looked upon the village from this tree, before our attack.

I remember lying in the cavity between the path and the riverbank, listening to the enemy speak of their plans to attack Ferocious Wind's village. I know that the enemy had every intention of destroying her people, and that explains a lot, but it doesn't make it easier for me to accept my part in the carnage. The waves of violence seem to ebb and flow between them. It has gone on for so long, nobody knows how it started. Initially, there must have been an aggressor, but it no longer matters. I know I'm destined to relive that horrible day, endlessly. In my memory, I can see things I didn't see in the moment. Perhaps my imagination has added the dark fog that surrounded the village that morning, or the tiny red pairs of dots that glowed from bright to dark. I have the feeling of flapping wings, like an unseen bat at dusk.

It is hard to push the dark thoughts away, so close to the grieving village. I need to rest. I wish I could be rid of the haunting grief that comes from that fateful day. I close my eyes and wrap my arms around the tree branch as if I am giving it a hug. That feeling I had under the hemlock tree comes to me again, only it is much more powerful. My spirit is attached to the tree, just as my body is. I feel myself under the surface of its bark. I'm small, small as a speck. I'm flowing through the tree, through its liquid tunnels. I'm surprised at how bright it is inside the tree, as if being inside a tree weren't astonishing enough in its own right. The liquid carries me to the outer branches, and then I'm pulled back through the branches into the trunk. Then I shoot deep down into the roots. I never imagined that I would be able to see beneath the surface of the ground. It's as if the dirt in the ground has disappeared. I can see the enormity of the tree is at least as massive beneath the ground as the branches that touch the sky. Tiny underground mushrooms decorate the roots. I feel like I can sense the affect they have on the roots, and it's a gently, delightful tickling sensation. Each is glad to have the other.

Underground, the roots of one tree tangle into the roots of the next. I feel myself speeding from one tree to the next. I wonder how far I am from the branch where my body rests. Perhaps it's a mile away. Each tree seems to have a unique presence, just as it is with people, only there is no evil within them. If someone were to tell me that plants and trees lived in this manner, I would have thought they were mad. As I travel the network of branches and roots, I no longer feel like a speck within the tunnels. I'm able to see, or at least sense the wild beauty and the vast distance of this new land compared to the little island I call home, or the bigger, emerald green island nearby.

Instead of a mile from my body, I'm aware that I'm dozens of miles, then hundreds of miles away. I can see the ocean where I washed ashore. I can see the tops of great mountains. I zip from here to there, moving quicker than fire up a twig, along rivers, past ponds, around lakes, and then thousands of miles away, carried from trees through blades of grass to another ocean, far, far away, then back again.

At the top of a great mountain, I sense my arrival at the topmost point of a gnarled, ancient tree that is no taller than I am. I feel its tortured, windblown existence as its seasons speed by in fast forward, its brittle limbs like the bones of a skeleton, and I feel the tiny feet of a small rodent scamper across its lowest branches and the tail that trails behind it before it jumps to the branch of another old tree nearby.

The top of the mountain looms above. I'm drawn to the treeless summit by tiny hair-sized roots of alpine flora, and my spirit answers the call as if it is sucked by the pull of a thousand magnets. I hang above the top of the mountain, floating effortlessly, and gazing out over a landscape of mountains, lakes, rivers and drifting clouds. I'm aware of a potent force that connects the world's highest places, like the netting that Fish Basket and Loon Feather make from cordage. My spirit glides from the top of the stately mountain and I feel like I'm seeing the world from the heavens. Is this the view of the world that God enjoys gazing upon? I soar across an ocean so vast, I'm amazed at its expansiveness. I'm certain that it is the wide ocean that I traversed by accident, and my suspicion is confirmed when I find myself hovering atop Skellig Michael, an answer to my homesick prayers. I greedily absorb the glory of the view in every direction. From there, I'm bounced around the planet. There are taller, more impressive mountains than the first two I encountered, but none that I'm more drawn to spiritually. It isn't just rocky mountain tops, I'm also transported to megalithic structures, from a circle of tall stones on a hillside on an island near my home to a trio of massive pyramids in the desert, to strange enormous boxes on a dry, high mountain plateau.

I wonder how long my spirit has been separated from my body. Is it safe to spend this much time away? Maybe my spirit belongs among the roots and branches of trees instead of inside a human body.

I speak with plants and I'm answered by spirits. "Become one with the botanical world. *We* can sustain your spirit, but your life must be lived within the flesh and blood of your human body. *We* can't tell you what to do, what to be, what to do, or where to go, but we can help you find the answer within yourself."

My spirit wonders, where am I now?

"This is the light within enlightenment."

I must know, how do I get back to my body?

Now I'm floating, weightlessly, like a cloud in the sky, only I'm in the familiar dream, my red and pink dream. A red vine is attached at my naval and I'm pulling at the vine, like I am pulling a fish through the water toward the shore. My spirit has returned to my body. It is morning. I untie myself from the branch I'm bound to. I look out over the view between the branches. I hear a reassuring voice within me. *Go now.*

On the ground, I set out through the virgin woodlands, skirting Bobcat Mask's village, safely picking up the trail again, well to the north of it.

As I trudge through the unexplored forest, I reflect on the journey of my soul the night before. Was it real? Are such things possible? Or was it just a dream? It was so vivid; how could it just be a conjuring created by my imagination?

In order to clear my way, I need to strike a path through the thick woods. I have the perfect instrument. I brandish my warclub like a sword, only I know the trees feel no pain as they're separated from the dead, dry twigs that stubbornly cling to their trunks. I leave a tunnel through the woods that reminds me of the tunnels beneath the bark of a tree.

It's slow going and my arm is tired. I take an early afternoon break at the side of a sparkling creek in a rocky clearing. I sit and lean against a gray boulder and listen to the sound of water flowing over rocks. A few feet away a perfectly shaped rock catches my attention. How is it possible for a rock to be perfectly shaped by nature? It's shaped like a puffin's egg. I stare at it intently, like it is the only object on earth, desperately hoping that it will hatch, and a tiny puffin will burst from its core. Instead it rises slowly from the ground. It hovers two feet above the ground, then it floats toward me. I hold out my hand, and it drops into my palm. I close my fingers around the cold rock and I realize that it fits perfectly within my grasp, like it was made for my hand, like the handle of my warclub. I look up into the heavens. What am I to make of this miracle?

I take a deep drink and fill my flask with water before heading back into the thick woods across the creek. With my club in my dominant right hand and the puffin egg in my left hand, I bore my way through the woods until dusk slows my path. I stir chunks of mushrooms into water and call it stew.

As I lay, tired and ready for sleep, I stroke the smooth surface of the rock egg, and I wonder, Why? Who am I? What will I become, and what will become of me? Where shall I go, and how will I know when I get there? I know the voice has the power to answer. It has spoken to me before. It is silent tonight. Perhaps the answer is in my hands, quite literally. I'm not a monk and I'm not a warrior. What am I? I am a mason. Perhaps that's why I hold a miracle in the form of stone.

Now that I know I am a mason, I have to figure out how to become one. I can fashion a mallet easily enough. The skills I acquired during endless winter nights fashioning warclubs will help me in that regard. How can I make chisels from nothing? I search my memory for fragments of knowledge on the subject of metallurgy. It will take some experimenting. I shall keep an eye out for likely looking rocks, and sources of sand and clay. In the meantime, I can place rock beside rock, fitting them together as closely as possible in their natural forms. I remember the small, dome-shaped huts we made at Skellig Michael. The end of my day of travel comes fast, and in my mind I've built a village of beehive-shaped huts. A village that I will occupy alone. I remember that I am banished, forever alone. How many stone huts am I likely to need?

As I'm preparing another bowl of hot water and mushrooms, I realize that I'm doing so one-handed. I'm still carrying that rock, and I have been all day. Every bit of weight is a burden when you're traveling long distances, but I can't resist the need to possess it. I unpack my travel basket and place the oval rock at the bottom, very reverently, as if it is an egg with a fragile shell.

I don't know how far I've come. It might seem like an ordinary day of minimal accomplishment, but for the miracle of the floating rock, the wonder of a world where everything is connected, the clarity of knowing who I am, and the realization that I have fashioned a sense of purpose. I shall survive the wilderness. I shall commune with the flora, I shall find a great mountain, and I shall work with stone. I needn't worry about why. Additionally, I shall pray more. I haven't done enough of that since the raging storms set me adrift on the vast ocean. I feel myself fully relax and I awake at dawn, fully rested and feeling content. The weight of worry has slipped from my shoulders.

Chapter 14

The next morning, I find a large creek or small river that is conveniently heading north. I'm able to move fast along its path. Rather than blaze myself a trail through dead branches, I sometimes need to weave my way through deadfall, sometimes climbing over trees that have fallen across the creek and sometimes crawling under them, though that's hard to do with a wide pack basket and a bow and arrows strapped onto my back.

Moving feels good. Moving fast feels productive. But as the day goes on, the settled feeling I have enjoyed fades slowly like gray clouds gradually darkening the sky after a sunny morning. I feel like I'm being followed and I feel like I'm being watched. Something behind me pushes me forward, faster and faster. I get a sense that I'm being chased.

I see a modest hemlock at the side of the creek ahead. The airy lace of its soft feathery needles allows tiny spots of sunlight to filter through to the forest floor. I have the feeling of rushing to the side of a waiting friend in a world in which I've known so few friends. I walk briskly to its side and place my open hands on the rough surface of its trunk.

I feel the kindly presence of the monk that served as father and mother to me. I see the ridge of dirty blond hair that encircles his head, contrasting with baldness above and beneath the ridge of hair.

The tonsure symbolizes his commitment to the values that he holds most precious, faith and humility. I bow my head, and I feel the tingling at my fingers. I try to clear the fears from my mind and prepare to receive whatever guidance I can get from the spirit of the tree that reminds me of Lector Beccán.

I see a dark silhouette against a foggy background, picking its way down a path through a tunnel in the woods. Someone pursues me and follows in the path I left through the woods. I can't recognize the shape of the person that is tracking me. Is it a precise vision, or is it a generalized warning? Am I being pursued by one person or a group of people? Whoever follows, I must not be found. I must travel, day and night. I wonder how far behind they are.

I opt for speed over silence, moving as fast through the river as I can. If I am being followed, my tracker must be ever careful to examine both sides of the creek to see if I have left the shelter of anonymity that it provides. At a point where the river bends toward the west, a rocky hillside to the north provides me an escape from the river from which I think I might disguise my exit. I leave nothing more than wet footprints on the stone, footprints which will quickly dry in the early autumn breeze. Beyond the rocky hill, I find a place where a long meadow meets the edge of a forest. I walk along the woods so I neither leave a trail of broken branches nor a parting of the grasses that would show I've walked through the meadow. If I haven't lost my tracker, I've certainly slowed them down. I smile, pleased with myself. Perhaps I can survive as a wild man.

As I continue on, I feel the spirit of my childhood guardian with me still, though I have left the hemlock tree miles behind me. Lector Beccán urges me forward, jostling my distracted mind, just as he did when I daydreamed rather than studying my lessons as a child. I hasten along, following a gentle tug, due north. I feel my teacher's commitment to serving our creator. I note a sense of irony as his message of pacifism is pushed. I must move fast and I must move far. My escape from the warrior's path is not certain. I don't know whether I'm followed still, or whether I've lost them, but the presence of my friend urges me forward. I hear Lector Beccán's voice as if he is whispering in my ear, "Hurry."

As I quicken my pace, my heart picks up speed and thoughts crowd my head. I wonder, what I'm doing here, why must I suffer so, and how is all of this possible? Why must I strive to survive in the wild among violent people whose only purpose seems to be the complete annihilation of each other? Why can't they let me go?

I recall seeing a waterspout above the surface of the ocean one day while I was lost, like a spinning cyclone, trying to grow into a tempest, a tempest that pulls everything inward into its core. I just want to live a passive life of prayer, and to be at one with the powers of the universe, connected to my creator and all of eternity.

Then it dawns on me. I will pray for *them*—these bitter woodland enemies. I can hurry northward and pray at the same time. I will pray endlessly, even at the risk of annoying God. He shall see my commitment and desire for these people to find a peaceful path forward. "Dear Lord, please let these rancorous foes find it within themselves to set aside their ancient hatreds. They have so much in common, they have no idea how similar they are." I only spent a few days among Bobcat Mask's raiding party, but aside from wearing different hues of paint, they're no different from Spits Teeth's people. I recall Three Fingers's account of Spits Teeth's captivity and the mutilation of Bobcat Mask's face. I know peace between these people is a big request, it's the sort of miracle that only God can deliver. "I pray, Heavenly Father, please help Bobcat Mask and Spits Teeth and their people."

The end of another day is upon me. I'm hungry. Hungry like I can't recall since being lost at sea. My last hearty meal was a belly full of blueberries. Aside from that, all I've had for days is mushrooms and water. I need more than that to sustain the effort of exertion that begins before dawn and often continues beyond sunset. How far must I go to lose myself in these woods? How far north is far enough? When will I find the mountains that I seek?

I must find a meal. I consider my bow, and hunting for deer. I consider the hooks and cordage that Ferocious Wind placed in my basket when I was banished. I decide that fishing is more likely to provide quick sustenance. I sit on a cold rock at the edge of the river, trying to tempt a fish with a hastily dug worm. The water is still. I haven't seen any sign of fish jumping at bugs on the surface. I stretch out on the face of the rock and stare into the water. I can see a good sized fish is mildly interested in the little red worm that twists and writhes, hoping to escape the hook that impales its body. My belly grinds painfully. I look at the fish and salivate. Frozen, motionless, I watch, desperately hoping. I attempt to will the fish to open its mouth, hungry or not, and take my bait. It seems like he swims from beneath his rock hundreds of times. I lust for the taste of his flesh. In my mind, I declare my need, and I offer God a prayer, "Dear Lord, if it pleases you, could you deliver me a meal to sustain me so that I may endure?" I grind my teeth together and imagine that I have the power to pry the fish's mouth open with the power of intense concentration. He has hit my line. I wait a fraction of a second and jerk the line, delicately, hoping to set the hook.

Tears of joy stream down my face. I hold a nine-inch trout in my hand, and I think of my puffin friend with fish hanging from either side of his bright beak. The slippery fish bends back and forth, still trying to escape back into its watery haven. I step away from the river, just in case he does manage to free himself from my grip.

It's amazing how easy it is to take food for granted when it's plentiful or provided by someone else. Having to find it myself and having to accept the uncertainty of relying on the providence of nature makes me appreciate a meal all the more. I'm being tracked, and I don't have time to coax a fire from my drill. I whack the fish in the head with a rock, then separate his head and guts from his body with my knife. I wash him in the river that was his home, and then I eat him raw. I think of what he would taste like cooked on a rock by a fire. One good thing about Tends Hearth, she knows how to make a meal taste good. I lick my fingers clean. Despite the unpleasant taste of uncooked trout, my belly rejoices at the fullness. It's great to be satiated. I thank God for delivering a meal I so gravely needed.

Nearby, a giant Buttonball tree dominates the landscape. Before it becomes completely enveloped in darkness, I hurry to stand in its shadow. I stretch my arms wide and realize that five people holding hands couldn't stretch their collective arms around the old tree. I look up into its massive canopy just as a spiky seedpod falls from above. The bark of the tree is a mottled pattern of gray, green, and beige, like the patterns that lichens leave on a rock as they compete for surface area. Lately, it seems, I'm becoming much more knowledgeable about the characteristics of the trees that surround me.

Again, I see a dark scene. Someone's silhouette slowly moves along a creek bed, bent at the waist, searching for clues. I realize they're looking for rocks displaced by the movement of feet beneath the surface of the river. This tracker is an expert. It would seem that their pace has slowed dramatically. In the distance, the old tree shows me the outline of a group of people moving through the dark tunnel in the forest. Perhaps the one ahead is a scout and the ones behind are the raiding party. Why do they seek me? There must be a more valuable use of the precious days that remain before the coming of winter.

It's hard to know how much of such images are true, actionable information, and how much is symbolically important. I must consider the possibilities. What if they are able to catch up with me? Should I surrender? Should I fight? If that should happen, I will have already failed at outrunning them and hiding from them. How many days have I spent promising myself and my maker a future of pacifism and prayer?

It would seem that I have increased the distance between myself and them. I recommit myself to my plan of run, hide, and if all else fails, surrender. How can I further obfuscate my trail?

By now, my pursuers must have realized that I am heading north. Perhaps they wouldn't expect me to change direction. My tingling fingertips on the flaky bark of the Buttonball tree register a negative response. I'm rarely aware of so direct an answer from the essence of trees. Words, clearly recognizable appear in my brain. "No, continue northward."

Perhaps the next time I come to a pond or a lake, I can swim across it. I twist my lips at the thought. I'm strong and I can swim, but how am I going to swim my pack basket across a lake? Perhaps I could walk into the lake, and then circle its perimeter along the shore. That might help me shake their tracking efforts.

I send a message of gratitude through my fingertips into the ancient tree and hurry off in a northerly direction, as instructed. Before long, I come to a large lake. I can barely see the end of it to the north. I hurry into the cold water, waist deep, grimacing when the cold water hits me beneath my breechcloth. I don't know how long I can withstand the cold. After a short distance, a creek spills into the lake and trails to the west. I need to get out of the lake, so I follow the creek for half an hour before leaving the creek and heading north again. At some point, I'll make up for the detour by spending an equal amount of time heading east.

I know I should travel through the night if I can, but I'm cold and tired. I search for a concealed spot, gather some firewood, a glob of pine resin, and some fluffy dry tinder from my basket. I spin my drill between my open palms and spark a flame in the tinder. The flammable resin helps the flame grow. My fire is at the base of a large pine tree, and I hope that its wide spreading branches will diffuse the smoke from my fire. I set water to heat and I look forward to hot mushroom stew for a change. My travel clothes dry by the fire and I wrap myself up in my old green monk's robe. I slip my hand into the interior pocket and remove my medallion.

I had forgotten my treasure. Until the egg-shaped rock dropped into my hand, the metallic spiral medallion had been my only valuable possession. It had been my mother's. Perhaps it had been her only treasure as well. Lector Beccán had placed the object in my hands on my seventh birthday and wrapped my fingers around the object that had been precious to my mother. My guardian told me that my mother's last words had been, "If my son should happen to survive, do please give this to him, so he will know that I will love him always."

When I hold it, I sorely miss the mother I never met and wish that I had the chance to glance upon her face, even just once. I love to trace the triple spirals with the tips of my fingers, following its continuous loop. It's a simple thing to do, and it makes me feel like my tiny existence means something, though I'm a tiny speck of a spot within the vast expanse of the universe. I return my medallion to its safe, hidden pocket and sleep for a couple of hours before I awaken to the bright light of the moon, halfway through the night. It is bright enough to travel, and I jump up from the ground, anxious to set my feet in motion again.

Chapter 15

The bright night feels serene. I enjoy a moonlight walk through the woods and I feel like I'm separating myself from my followers.

By morning, things change. Clouds roll in as the sun rises, and the temperatures slowly drop. As the day passes, my unsettled feeling becomes more ominous. I recall the curse, the curse on my mother, the curse on her descendants, and more specifically, the curse on my birth.

The black foggy feeling I remember from the day of the attack on Bobcat Mask's village follows me now. Periodically, I turn to see if it has dissipated, but it rolls through the landscape behind me. Is it a warning? An omen? Is it indicative of something bad to come, or is it the something bad I have been warned about?

I walk up a hill and into a meadow that is home to a handful of trees. I feel my jaw drop as I look from tree to tree. Each tree has a giant vertical slash in its trunk. It looks like a giant otherworldly bear has scratched the trees with its horrifying claws. I hurry to the nearest one and touch the bottommost part of its scar. I quickly pull my hand back, like when I accidentally touch a hot rock at the edge of the fire. I close my eyes and place my hands on either side of the scar. I'm transported back through time to a horrible storm with frantic winds and lightning that struck the trees and shook the ground. The fire burned within the trunk of the tree for half an hour before the swirling winds and driving rains smothered the fire. Each tree was hit by a direct bolt of lightning. I think of Tends Hearth and the tree-shaped pattern on her back.

I feel myself pulled into this wounded tree. From inside, I can see that its essence has found a way to bypass its damaged section. I travel down its trunk to the roots beneath the ground. This tree and its four sisters radiate subterranean beauty. Their root structures are ten times larger than their canopies. The magnificent spread of amber-colored roots glows with the twinkle of a billion luminescent fungi. As I move from root to root and tree to tree, I feel like I'm shooting through the sky at midnight and bouncing off the stars. Each little twinkle tickles me like it tickles the roots of the trees, enriching them and providing them the nutrients they need. I feel a blast of hopefulness expand within my chest. I tumble around weightlessly, tossed like a leaf in the river.

After a while, my spirit is passed from root to root. I find myself beneath the tree where I lit a fire to warm my wet clothes by the lake. There are six painted warriors bent over the remains of my fire. Fear quickly replaces the hopefulness in my heart. The man in the ugly cat mask squats by my dead fire and scoops the coals into his hand. He drops the coals fast. They must still be hot. He smells his fingers, as if the coals can tell him what I might have cooked over the fire. I try to calculate how long ago I was there.

I'm disappointed. I've been careful and I've moved so fast. How is it possible they have been able to find my trail? It is urgent that I increase my speed. A feeling of panic pierces my chest, and I'm snapped back into my body. I pull my pack basket to my shoulders and start to run as if I'm running for my life. I can't escape the sense of foreboding and the feeling that I am doomed. I feel like a rabbit or a deer, creatures that live their lives in fear, knowing that everything wants to hunt, kill, and eat them. I'm being stalked, like prey.

The hills have grown steeper. At this point, they've become mountains rather than hills. My legs are strong, and my muscles remember the years I spent traveling up and down the steep inclines at Skellig Michael. I trot up creek beds that must be raging rivers in the spring. In the autumn, most of them are dry as bones. In the distance, I see mountains that look impressive, even compared to my memory of home.

Late in the afternoon, I traverse the side of a mountain with exposed rock, certain that I am leaving no trail that can be followed. I wonder how much time and distance it will take before they give up the chase. I look to the top of the mountain. I wonder, would they look for me there? I am tempted. I would love to look out at the world from that vantage point. But I can't risk it. I can get farther faster by skirting the mountain. I would love to stop here and make this mountain my home, but evidently, I am not far enough away from the feuding villages. I can't stay here.

I look back up the hill, and I see enormous boulders balanced on the edge of the mountainside. I wonder what it would take to move those boulders. I fantasize that I'm taunting the war party from above those rocks. What if I could push the rocks down upon them as they scale the face of the mountain? Though they look like they hang precariously; they must be more permanently affixed to the side of the mountain, or they would have come crashing into the valley below, a long time ago.

Pebbles roll from the base of the boulders. They are followed down the mountain by a shower of gravel. I stare hard at the boulders above. My arms start to shake and my head hurts. With every fiber of my being, I want those rocks to stay as they are. I can't divert my gaze. Things are happening so fast.

I feel the earth shake beneath my feet, and I fear that the earth will open and swallow the mountain above me. I hear a familiar voice in my head. *Run. Get away. Fast.*

The muscles in my legs have tightened, but I realize that I must go. I shouldn't have lingered here so long. My legs have received the message from my aching brain. I scramble to get away from the mountain, my eyes still on the boulders above. The giant rock above begins to fall, as if it were pushed by the invisible hand of the giant bear that scratched the trees.

My legs move as fast as they will go. My mouth is dry. I wish I could transport myself magically into the forest that I can see beyond the rocky mountainside. I've stopped looking at the falling rock so I can concentrate on my escape. In my mind, I can still see the boulder crashing down the side of the mountain, only time has slowed, even as my heartbeat has quickened.

The world has gone dark.

I don't know how long I've been out. My head is throbbing. My mouth is so dry, my tongue feels like rough bark. I open my eyes and my body is all scratched up, like a scraped knee from a childhood fall, only across my whole body. I can't see my left foot. It's buried beneath a pile of gravel and a rock the size of my head sits on top of it. I sit up and slide toward my left foot. Adrenaline shoots through my body. I shove the rock aside and dig away at the gravel. I must get my foot out.

Finally, I have uncovered my foot. Using both hands, I pick up my left foot and place it next to my right foot. I reach for my pack basket. As I pull it toward me, it falls apart. I pick among the rubble and remains of the basket and pocket a few fishhooks. The food and water I have been carrying are gone. I have nothing else except my knife. The loss of my possessions almost breaks my heart. What I'm missing most is the rock that is shaped like a puffin's egg. That, and the spiral medallion. Instead, I should be mourning the loss of my bow and arrow.

I remember that I'm being chased and I jump to my feet and take one step before my body collapses. My left foot hurts as much as my throbbing head. I put my hand on the back of my head. There's no blood, but my touch increases the pain. I can't think of that now. I have to make my foot move beneath me.

My fingers explore the scrapes and scratches on my foot. I can't find evidence of broken bones. I convince myself that it is just a twisted ankle. Slowly I rise to my feet again, putting all of my weight on my right foot. My left foot barely holds my weight as I hobble from the mountainside into the woods. I think of my pack basket. My pursuers will know exactly what happened on this mountainside. I pray that they will think my remains lie beneath a pile of rock, somewhere below.

As I reach the forest, it feels like it took me a week to get there. I look back at the aftermath of the avalanche, then I freeze and listen. I hear the sound of running water, gentle, like a brook or stream rather than a raging river. My mouth feels like it is full of wood and splinters. The sound of the brook gives me hope in the midst of a situation that I increasingly think of as hopeless.

The feeling of being followed begins building within my chest again. I hobble through the thick woods as quickly as I can, pulled along by the sound of the stream. I long to dip my head under the surface and let the cool water into my mouth.

Pain shoots through my body with every step. The throbbing ache at the back of my head competes for attention with my swollen ankle that barely supports my attempt to escape. I remember the sound of the bear crashing through the woods near the blueberries, and I wonder if my passage through the forest sounds the same. I can't hear the branches break around me because my mind can only hear the brook ahead. It grows slightly louder as I limp along. What I thought might take a few minutes seems vastly longer.

Finally, I break out of the woods and there it is. A glorious ribbon of water. I hobble to its side as fast as I can. I carefully lower my body to the soft dirt at the side of the creek. I feel as if my prayers have been answered as I splash water onto my face. Then I cup my hands together and drink from the bowl my hands create. I know I should start with a little, then try a little more. Water never tasted so good. I drink a little bit more, then I slide toward the creek, fill my cheeks and lungs with a deep breath of air and dip my head beneath the surface of the water. I keep my head underwater as long as I can. Half a minute later, I pull my head from the creek and rub the excess water from my eyes. Then I roll to a sitting position and swing my club of a foot into the cold water. I'm aware of how painfully cold the water is and I feel my toes begin to numb, yet I know the water is helping my ankle. I stretch my body on the creek bank and look up into the sky above the tiny meadow at the side of this lifesaving creek. I'm grateful for its presence, but I know I am not safe yet. I wonder, will I ever feel safe again? What shall I do next? How long can I keep going? I can't think of anything else to do. I must flee or hide. There is no other plan. Unless it is surrender.

As I gaze into the gray sky above, I'm aware that something is falling from the sky. It isn't rain. First there is just a flake, then others follow behind it. I've seen snow before, so I don't know why I'm so surprised to see it today. I can't remember ever having been on my back, watching snow fall from the sky. A flake lands on my nose and melts on impact. Normally, I would have marveled at the wonder of the snow falling from the sky, but today I think, this can't be good. It's too early in the season for snow, isn't it?

The feeling of being hunted returns. I take another quick drink of water from the creek, wishing there is a way I could carry some with me. I head forward, not knowing exactly what direction I'm traveling. I must let the fates choose for me.

Am I being tested?

Chapter 16

The terrain is rocky and I pass through alternating forests and meadows. I can tell that it will be dark soon. I've been looking around for any likely spot to find some comfort in the night. Ideally, I'd like to find a hemlock tree with thick low branches that conceal the ground at its base. I've taken comfort from the shelter they provide on other nights.

I would have settled for less than ideal spots, but I have the feeling that the enemy is closing in on me. I don't know whether it is my head playing tricks on me, or whether my feet can feel it from vibrations of the ground beneath my feet. I feel sick to my stomach with worry. I know I have no weapons, and I wonder if I have any will to fight if confronted. My mind is beginning to accept that I shall have to surrender and beg for mercy, when something violently crashes onto my back. I feel sharp claws dig into the backs of my arms and thighs, and I am aware of giant teeth at my shoulder.

I remember Ferocious Wind telling me to withdraw from the presence of a bear but to fight back if I'm attacked by a cat. I know that I must break free of the attack, stand, scream, and fight. I can feel the massive weight of the cat pressing me into the ground, flattening me. As blackness overtakes me, the last thought that crosses my mind is that I have been smothered.

I am aware of darkness all around me and it is quiet. Empty and quiet. Worry has left me. I don't know if I am hanging, floating, or lying on some unseen surface. I am grateful to have escaped the fears that have gripped me for so long. In the distance, I see a tiny white spot that slowly grows. It begins to twinkle, like a single star in a sky of black.

The white light grows and grows, gradually replacing the darkness. Instead of emptiness, I feel surrounded by a sense of hope and wonder. I am savoring a feeling of acceptance and validation. Then I begin to be aware of another sensation within my core. It feels warm and comforting. A tumbling feeling replaces the feeling of weightlessness and I'm enveloped in reds and pinks again. I hear some sort of cosmic music I can't describe, but I feel that tugging sensation again.

My eyes flutter open. It's dark and I see a single star in the black sky. Every part of my body hurts. I turn my head slightly. I feel the warmth of red, orange, and yellow flames from a fire close by. Beside the fire, I see the dead body of a massive cat. I can see its fierce face. Its eyes are closed and its mouth is gaping. Its face conveys its intent—to slam its teeth into its prey—me. It isn't the face of a bobcat that I'm looking upon. It is bigger, and even more frightening. I gaze down the length of the massive mountain lion. It must be twice my weight and size, perhaps more. I notice three arrows sticking out of its side. How is this possible? I was attacked from behind, and aside from that, I lost my bow and arrows in the avalanche.

Then I see a silhouette in the darkness at the edge of the clearing. Someone is there. Perhaps they have saved me from the attack of the horrifying creature. I'm aware of the cracking sounds of twigs and branches breaking. Someone is gathering wood to feed the fire. My eyes are adjusting to the darkness. I'm surprised to see that it is a woman. She approaches the fire with some wood. It hurts to speak, but I can't help myself. "Have you been following me?"

She speeds to my side, kneels carefully on the blanket beneath me, and gently touches her lips to mine. There's a look of relief on her face. Her usual ferocious countenance has been replaced by the bright look of love that reminds me of the twinkle of the star in the darkness that had surrounded me just moments earlier.

"It hasn't been easy to find you. Sure, sometimes it was hard to miss your trail, but at other times, it was most difficult. There were times I thought I'd never find you. It's a good thing I'm an expert tracker." She presses her lips gently against my lips again as I close my eyes.

I don't know how long I have slept, but it is fully daylight when I wake again. I am surrounded by a hastily constructed, open-faced structure overlooking the fire a few feet away. Strips of meat drip over the fire and the head of the mountain lion looks back at me from the top of a rock, a short distance from the fire. The hair on the back of my neck prickles. It is as if I can feel the hot breath of the cat on my neck, moments before its teeth puncture my skin, its body crunches my bones, and its claws spill my blood. In the midst of the attack, I couldn't have been aware of such details. Lying by the fire with the cat's head separated from its body, I relive the tiny details of the attack. I can sense the cat waiting for the right moment to pounce on me, and its hot panting breath. The memory of the rancid smell of its breath, a cross between the smell of rotting meat and the spray of a skunk, permeates my nasal cavities. It's a wonder how the thought or memory of a smell has the same power as the actual smell itself.

As I look at the hideous face that was moments from shredding my body into strips of meat like the ones that are drying over the fire, I wonder how many of these beasts roam the mountains. Why must the world be so full of danger at every turn? I've never been more aware of a desire for a placid existence.

I feel like I should get up, so I start to gather the strength of my muscles to rise from the ground. My slightest effort is met with pain from head to toe. I lie still, and I'm aware of the throbbing at the back of my head. My ankle still pulses with pain. The wounds on my arms and legs sting and itch at the same time. My head feels hot and I feel like my blood carries poisonous fire throughout my body.

My eyes flutter as Ferocious Wind tiptoes into the clearing, carrying water from the stream. My fluttering eyes are the only part of my body that don't seem to hurt when I move them. Despite my pain-racked body, my heart is filled with wonder and gladness for this woman, my warrior woman. How could I have left her behind? I'm so grateful that she has followed me. She sees that I am awake and she dashes to my side.

Ferocious Wind pours some water onto a patch of moss and places it on my forehead. "You have the fever. Your head is hot. I've been trying to cool you down." With the compress on my forehead, she places cool, wet patches of moss on my wrists. "I can't think of anything else to do," she apologizes as she places the soggy blobs of moss across my chest and on my thighs where the blood is carried from my core to my legs. I feel my skin tingle and my heart leap. I close my eyes, pray for my survival, and try to forget the feeling of her fingers on my thighs.

Perhaps hours have passed. I feel water dribbling from the corners of my mouth. I swallow greedily, and I feel more water being squeezed into my mouth. My head feels like it is on fire. I open my eyes and it is hard to focus. I try to talk, but I can hear that my words are jumbled sounds, not words. I don't even know what I'm trying to say.

I'm glad to see the woman at my side, but I'm concerned about the look on her face. Her lips quiver and tears are running down her cheeks. I can't remember ever having seen fear on the brave face of this beautiful woman. My warrior woman. "You must fight, Conchobar. Will you fight for me?"

I know my words don't make sense and I can't control the movement of my body, but I hope she understands that I will fight as hard as I can.

With her hand behind my neck, she tilts my head and puts a wooden spoon in my mouth. The hot meat-flavored broth fills my mouth. Each swallow feels like a day of hard labor. After a couple of dozen swallows, she sets my head back down on the blanket on the ground. I close my eyes and go to sleep, tired, as if I have been awake for days instead of minutes.

Again, I'm aware of my aching head, suddenly comforted by pressure above my eyebrows. My eyes blink open and I tilt my head. Ferocious Wind is at my side, her face twisted with worry. I hear her words again, "Fight for me, Conchobar."

I feel myself nodding. I wonder if my head really is moving. Even if it isn't, I know that my eyes are moving up and down within my eye sockets. The slightest movement requires all the effort I can muster. Again, I am not able to form words.

Ferocious Wind reaches for a bowl at the edge of the fire and tilts my head again for more soup. I feel my skin tingle as my body begins to absorb sip after sip. Protein, fat, and water. I feel the power of the mountain lion's meat and I'm able to form words again.

"How long have I been like this?"

"It has been two days." Ferocious Wind sniffles and doesn't try to hide the tears on her cheeks. "I was afraid I had lost you."

I think I'm smiling as I answer. "I'm stronger than I look."

It looks like she is stifling the urge to laugh even as she cries. I can see that she has been busy during the last two days. There are mounds of wood piled around the fire. The enormous pelt of the massive lion is staked on the side of the clearing. A light blanket of snow sparkles brightly as winter fights to replace autumn. Its approach is strengthening. The frame of a half-finished snowshoe sits at her side. Then I notice that the mask of the mountain lion has been separated from its skull, and the shelter that surrounds me has increased in size.

"You have been busy. I wish I could help." I feel like I'm frowning and I add, "I never should have left without you."

She reaches forward and strokes my hair. "I should not have let you go. I cannot let you go. I will not let you go."

I know that she is fighting for my survival even harder than I am. As if she hasn't done enough, an urgent request crosses my mind. "Can you save me the claws and the teeth?"

Ferocious Wind's eyebrows dance on her forehead, "I *have* saved them. They are to be my marriage present, if you'll have me."

"I don't have anything for you." My heart aches. I long for the future, a time beyond lying helplessly on the ground, fighting for my life.

"We'll worry about that later. Right now, you have to get stronger. I'll build us a winter home in this clearing."

I feel the gentle touch of her lips on my mouth again as the weight of my eyelids takes me back to the land of slumber. As my mind wanders into the hopes and dreams of our future together, I hear her voice urging me, once again, "Fight for me, Conchobar."

Chapter 17

I can hear the patter of the footsteps, the pads of the mountain lion's paws on the forest floor. The hot breath on my neck. The claws on the backs of my arms and my thighs. The hot breath on my neck. My eyes open and roll around within my eye sockets. I'm sweating and screaming.

People rush to my side. How is this possible? On some level, I am aware that I am delirious. I recall Ferocious Wind at my side. Who are these other people? I'm aware of them as a swirling blur. I don't know how many of them there are. Then I experience a falling sensation, like I am falling into a dark cone, a cone that is getting smaller and smaller, approaching its narrowest point. How can I fall beyond that point?

I awaken slowly and I hear voices nearby. Ferocious Wind has asked a question. A man answers. "The fever has broken." The voice is familiar, yet I can't place it. My mind wanders through the dissipating fog as I return to the realm of conscious thought and awareness.

Another man's voice adds sympathetic and comforting words with a deeper voice. I blink rapidly and moan, comforted by his presence. I recall his healing touch and the soothing sound of his voice. My vision crystallizes and I see Three Fingers standing between Ferocious Wind and Gathers Seeds.

I find my voice. "How did you find us?" I couldn't be more surprised if Lector Beccán were to materialize in the clearing. "Why? Why are you here?"

They come to my side. Three Fingers shushes me in his low voice. "We can talk about that later. Tell us how you feel."

I stammer to answer. I haven't thought about how I feel. "Better. Stronger, I think. Hungry. And thirsty, I guess." I glance down my body and my eyes widen in surprise. I've turned green and fuzzy. I blink in disbelief, spreading moisture in my eyes until I realize that I'm lying beneath a blanket of moss.

Gathers Seeds speaks, and I turn to look at him. "You gave us quite a scare, Conchobar."

"How did I get so sick? What do you think it is?"

He answers, "I think the mountain lion carried a poison on the tips of his teeth and the daggers of his claws. Your blood carried the poison throughout your body. I think we have healed the poison in your body, and I think Three Fingers has scared the evil spirit of the wild cat's soul away. Now you must get stronger."

Ferocious Wind holds forward yet another cup of meaty soup. Gathers Seeds pinches a generous helping of ground leaves and seeds from a woven bag. Ferocious Wind stirs the soup, while Three Fingers tilts my head forward. I can't remember anything ever tasting so good. I greedily slurp the soup, then ask for more. This seems to please my friends.

When I'm done, I realize that I'm cold, and I begin to shiver. Three Fingers and Gathers Seeds look at each other. I wonder what they're thinking, and Three Fingers turns to me and tells me he thinks it is a good sign. They begin to remove the moist moss from my body, and the movement of the air on my clammy skin makes me even colder. My skin is white and shriveled. As they uncover my nakedness, I feel self-conscious and I close my eyes. Finally, when the moss has been cleared away, a thick warm blanket is spread across my body and I feel more at ease. Gathers Seeds doubles the wood on the fire, and I can see that they have built a stone wall on the opposite side. The comforting warmth of the fire is directed toward the opening in the structure which has grown even more substantially around me. I wonder how long I was unconscious as I realize the structure is now large enough for four people to fit within it.

With the fever gone and the strength provided by the rich soup, I feel strong enough to stay awake. I want to know more. "You must tell me. How did you get here?"

My friends sit cross-legged by my side and they wrap blankets over their shoulders. Three Fingers places a hand on my arm. He looks across my body into Ferocious Wind's face and begins speaking. "After you left, Ferocious Wind moped around the village for a couple of days. We worried about her. She seemed heartbroken. Then one morning, she was gone. Missing. Vanished."

Three Fingers turns to his side and looks at his partner. "We knew right away she had left to find you." Three Fingers looks back at me and continues. "To join you. When Spits Teeth learned of her disappearance, he flew into a rage. With the death of his sons, the warrior daughter he had ignored for most of her life became immediately precious to him. We were present because the youngest boy, Struts Like a Goose, had broken his leg. It was quite a scene. Fish Basket wailed at the loss of the last of her children. Loon Feather doted over her son. Tends Hearth sat by the fire and sobbed. She hacked away the hair on her head in grief. She said it was all her fault, that she shouldn't have blamed you, Conchobar. She screeched at her father, telling him that it was his wickedness and warlike ways that had doomed her family. At that moment, I looked into Gathers Seeds's eyes and we both understood that Tends Hearth was right. We could no longer remain in that village. For how many generations have the people in our village struggled against the people in Bobcat Mask's village? The passing of time hasn't reduced the violence. With each passing year, our people have become weaker. There has to be something more to life. So whatever the outcome, we set out in a new direction, looking to follow a new way."

Gathers Seeds picks up the story for a while. "Spits Teeth raged." Gathers Seeds reaches across my body and briefly places his hand on Ferocious Wind's knee. "He told the council that first he would find you. Then you would help him lead the warriors into Bobcat Mask's village to finish them off, once and for all. Of course, Dancing Bear conjured up the blessing of the Great Spirit. Hole in the Roof refused to consent to the plan. Who knows what happened next?" Gathers Seeds shakes his head and raises his eyebrows. Then he puts his hand on Three Fingers's shoulder. "We gathered a few things and disappeared into the night. Sometimes I look back and wonder whether we should have stayed. We are not warriors. We are not meant to walk the wild lands alone. Somehow, Three Fingers talked me into leaving."

All the parts of the story and the possible future implications bounce around in my head. I'm left with the understanding that Spits Teeth will never stop looking for Ferocious Wind, nor will he ever give up on his desire to annihilate the enemy, even if every last member of his family and everyone in his village dies in the process. I should hate him, but I can't help feeling sorry for him. Try as I do, I can't fathom how the healers found us. I plead with them to tell me how they found us.

Though they protest, I can tell that Three Fingers is looking forward to telling this story. "You may have sensed that I have been increasingly critical of Dancing Bear. I have been a healer for many years and have left the visions to the seers. Only, since you arrived in our village, Conchobar, I have started having visions myself. And my visions often conflict with Dancing Bear's premonitions. Then one day, I realized that Dancing Bear makes up his visions to suit Spits Teeth's desires."

Gathers Seeds interrupts, suggesting that I need a drink of water. Ferocious Wind holds her bowl at my lips, and I greedily gulp the cool water. I can't wait to hear what comes next, and I quickly look back to Three Fingers, hoping that he will continue.

"So we set out in the middle of the night. If ever there were an opportunity to find out whether the Great Spirit wishes to communicate with me, this was it. We started out by happenstance, headed south." Three Fingers smiles knowingly at Gathers Seeds. "One hour down the path, everything seemed wrong. We turned around and headed in the opposite direction, and everything seemed right. We traveled for days, not knowing whether we were headed in the right direction, not sensing any guidance from the world of spirits. We knew that winter approaches, and we were ill equipped to face it. Then we found ourselves in a cleared tunnel within a very dark section of woods, to the north of Bobcat Mask's village. I felt the forest's memory of you, Conchobar, and then I felt the forest's memory of Ferocious Wind."

Three Fingers uncrosses and re-crosses his legs, with the opposite leg on top. "Since then, I have heard the whisper of the spirits of trees. We aren't too bad at tracking, and sometimes it was very easy. Sometimes it was very difficult. Whenever we were puzzled, all I had to do was approach a tree, and I felt an indescribable tug in one direction or another, but mostly north. There was one point where it seemed hopeless. We were on the side of a rocky mountain, and there weren't any trees nearby. Incredibly, I squatted on the side of a mountain and cupped the blades of a tiny yellowish green sedge in the palms of my hands, and from that tiny plant, I felt the strongest pull I had felt yet. Sometimes the greatest beauty exists within the smallest lifeforms. Ten minutes later, we were standing in the aftermath of an avalanche. Within the avalanche, we found some of your things, Conchobar, your green robe and the contents of its hidden pocket. The powerful symbol that protects you."

He pauses. Incredulously, I ask, "Protects me?" The notion contradicts my belief that I am cursed.

He continues, "With your robe and the symbol clutched to my chest, Conchobar, I started to feel your pain. I felt the mountain lion stalking you. It had been following you for days. I felt it spring into the air, and I felt its claws dig into your skin. I felt its teeth open and I felt the arrows that pierced its chest. I felt it land on you. I felt Ferocious Wind's hands roll its body off of you, and I felt her desperation as she tended to your wounds."

Three Fingers turns to Gathers Seeds and asks for the rock. Then Three Fingers looks at me and asks whether an egg-shaped rock is important to me. I nod, amazed that they found the rock and that they thought to carry it.

Three Fingers continues. "The vision also compelled us to bring this rock with us."

I tell them about the birds from home and how the rock reminds me of their eggs. I'm grateful that they brought it with them from the avalanche site.

Gathers Seeds speaks of their arrival in the clearing. "We found Ferocious Wind struggling to keep you alive. She might have managed to do it even without us. I don't think we've ever seen a fever like the one you had. The plants I brought didn't seem enough to save you, but the forest called Three Fingers to an alpine plant I am unfamiliar with. Three Fingers told me that the Great Spirit had sent him a message. So here we are. It looks like we have managed to cure you. Now we have to manage to survive the winter in this new little village."

It is an incredible story. I think about Three Fingers's ability to hear the thoughts of plants and trees. I wonder if he's aware of the full extent of their power. I think I'd like to ask him about that privately instead of with others around. My thoughts return to worry and I ask, "What about Spits Teeth and Bobcat Mask?"

My friends look at each other questioningly.

I continue. "Do you think they'll wait until spring? The way you describe it, it doesn't seem like they can wait that long to kill each other."

From the faces they make at each other, I can tell that they're unsure as well. We debate what to do next. Who knows what Spits Teeth and Bobcat Mask will do? Our first priority must be preparing for winter. It would be nice to have two shelters but there isn't time.

Food is our greatest priority, and we have one able-bodied hunter among us. Ferocious Wind seems to relish the thought and quickly embraces the challenge. "I shall be a hunter rather than a warrior." Moments later, she is gone.

Chapter 18

"I must get to my feet. Will you help me?" My friends look concerned.

Gathers Seeds scolds, "It is too soon. You must rest and get stronger first."

"There isn't time for that," I insist. I don't know how long it has been since I have stood on my feet. I've lost track of time. Stubbornly, I try to stand on my own.

Three Fingers runs to my side, and Gathers Seeds is right behind him. The act of standing makes me feel dizzy, and I feel a pounding in the back of my head. My ankle is still sore but I am able to stand on it. My muscles are weak and my legs wobble. At first, it seems that I have completely forgotten how to walk. Then my muscles seem to remember what is required of them. My friends steady me with their hands on my arms. After the tentative steps I take crossing the clearing, I ask them to release my arms. I limp back. They remain at my side, ready to catch me if I fall. I won't win any foot races, but I have proven that I can walk a short distance. "How far to the river?"

Gathers Seeds confesses that it isn't far and offers to take me there. After a slow, short stroll, we arrive at the river. It is early afternoon and the snow that fell the night before has long since melted. I lean against a birch tree beside the river, stroking the papery bark and tracing around the black marks that pock its surface. I long to dive beneath the surface of the thin bark. It might be better if my friends take a walk. “Have you foraged in this area? Maybe there are some mushrooms we can collect for the winter.”

Gathers Seeds insists that I rest while they explore. I decide that I’ll start out leaning against the tree, and if I grow tired, I’ll slide down and sit on the ground beneath it.

I’m surprised how quickly the tree draws me in and how quickly it shoots me through its trunk and roots, then off to its neighbor. I fly so quickly from tree to tree that I don’t feel a sense of enjoying the journey. From a tall tree at the edge of the woods, my spirit dangles from the tip of a tiny branch. Looking down is frightening, and I have a feeling in the pit of my stomach and a sense that I am falling. I prepare for the feeling of hitting the ground when something even more frightening comes into view. I see Bobcat Mask and his party of six at the avalanche where I twisted my ankle and bumped my head. I’m not sure if I’m actually seeing them, or if it is a vision of seeing them in the near future. I hang suspended for another moment, and then I feel the pull of the current of the tree tugging me back to where my body waits.

I return to my body with a snap and a pop that leaves me feeling weak. I slide down the trunk of the tree and rest at its base. My headache has returned. I stroke the back of my head, gently hoping that will ease the pain. I try to derive meaning from my vision. I understand that danger is on the way, but I can’t tell how soon.

When Three Fingers and Gathers Seeds return from a successful forage, I tell them about my vision. There isn’t time to tell them everything about the trees. We make our way back to the clearing. Everything is the way we left it except for the fire, which has died back. A dead porcupine lies beside the fire. Ferocious Wind must have secured the animal and then gone back out to see if she can bring in another kill. Gathers Seeds insists that I lay down and rest.

I am tired and I have no will to argue. They tell me that they're going down the path to see if they can see anything at the avalanche site. They'll try to be back by dark.

When I wake up, it is well after dark. My friends are busy digging a deep hole in the middle of the clearing. I struggle to my feet and wander over. They tell me they are making a ground cache to store food for the winter. They plan to build a cover with rocks and branches to keep the predators and scavengers from our winter stores. "What about the enemy," I ask, "did you see them?"

They reassure me that the enemy is not on the mountainside today. It's good to know they're not upon us yet. Clearly, what I experienced was a vision, not a view. "What shall we do? Is there anything we can do to prepare?"

My questions are answered with their questions. How many are there? Do you recognize the enemy? Perhaps the visions are from next summer.

I ask Ferocious Wind if we can make bows and arrows for everyone in the morning. I wonder if they believe me. While they dig the earth, I take a y-shaped branch from the firewood pile. Remembering Spits Teeth's instructions by the fireside, I send wood chips flying, making the fastest version of a war club I can. In two hours, I have a roughly hewn war club in my hand. It needs a lot of work, but in the meantime, if it were necessary, it could be used effectively.

The next morning, I'm feeling well enough to venture down the trail toward the avalanche site. From the edge of the woods, I survey the mountainside. On the way back, I gather saplings and willow branches. When I return to our clearing, I'm amazed at how many rocks and branches the healers have collected.

At the end of the day, Ferocious Wind returns with a basket full of venison and a deer hide. We work together to prepare strips of meat to dry over the fire and then we work on making our bows.

Nobody knows how long we'll have to prepare. Will the four of us be enough to defend against Bobcat Mask and his party of six? I hope we don't find out soon. We aren't ready. Ferocious Wind and the healers don't seem nearly as concerned as I am. I have a sick feeling at the pit of my stomach. I'm certain that I'm right. That feeling of being hunted, stalked, and tracked has returned. Last time I had that feeling, I was attacked by the mountain lion.

The next morning, I feel compelled to make another trip to the edge of the forest. Ferocious Wind walks with me, thinking she will hunt in that direction today. We hold hands through the meadows when the trail is wide enough. I'm getting stronger and require few breaks. On the way to the edge of the forest, we only stop twice.

At one break, I ask Ferocious Wind when we should marry. Neither of us wants to wait. It can't be soon enough. We agree to talk to Three Fingers and Gathers Seeds about it around the fire tonight. I think of the day we huddled together at the riverbank listening to Bobcat Mask and his hunting party. Again, the threat of Bobcat Mask hangs over us today. Nevertheless, we embrace. We kiss hungrily and I feel her hands on my back as my hands stoke her shoulders. We lose track of our surroundings and forget to remain vigilant, and we're surprised by the unexpected arrival of Three Fingers and Gathers Seeds.

Three Fingers clears his throat so that we will not be alarmed by their presence. Gathers Seeds tells us that they are just passing by on a foraging expedition. They don't linger. I notice that they join hands just before they disappear into the forest. I can only recall seeing them do that on one other occasion.

Ferocious Wind and I part awkwardly and we head off together toward the edge of the forest. Before we venture from the anonymity of the woods, we scan the horizon to make sure no one is visible on the side of the mountain or the trail beyond. We separate. Ferocious Wind follows the trail across the side of the mountain, back along the trail that led us all here and I turn back toward our clearing. I plan to spend the afternoon pulling fish from the river. A good supply of dried trout will add nicely to our winter stores.

All afternoon, at the side of the river, I look forward to gathering again at dusk. I wonder if Three Fingers and Gathers Seeds will be surprised by the plans Ferocious Winds and I have made. I wish we could go away alone together and unite without the possibility of being interrupted by a raiding party. I think of our embrace in the meadow and feel an ache in my chest. I am glad for the company of the healers, but I long for time alone with my beloved. I think of Spits Teeth and his wives. I hope that Ferocious Wind will be happy when we are intimate. I recall the sounds that Fish Basket and Loon Feather would make during and after coupling with Spits Teeth. I don't want to make Ferocious Wind feel hurt and I hope we have complete privacy when we are married, at least for a while. A fish hits my line and momentarily distracts me from thoughts of Ferocious Wind.

While waiting for another fish, I gaze at a rock on the other side of the river. I think of the rocks at the top the mountain before the avalanche sent them tumbling. I concentrate harder and harder on the rock in my sights. Surprisingly it begins to shake, then it rises from the position it has occupied, perhaps for eons. I tip my head back and the rock rises higher, six feet into the air before the shock of what has happened causes me to lose my concentration. The rock tumbles back to the ground, landing two feet from where it had been. How is this possible? I feel a cool breeze blow across my shoulder and gooseflesh rises on my skin. Another fish strikes my hook.

Perhaps it was a fluke. Can I do it again? I find another rock and concentrate. This one is even bigger than the prior rock, and it is sitting in the middle of the river. I lock my eyes on it and with the power of my thoughts, I silently command it to lift itself from the river. I wonder how high I can lift it. The rock rises six feet above the river and I tip my head farther back. The rock is twice as high as it was before. I shake my head from side to side in amazement, and the rock shifts back and forth above the water. I hadn't thought of that. I lose concentration and the rock falls into the river with a splash. I concentrate on the rock again and move it with my mind, placing it beside the other rock I lifted. It's a wonder that fish are biting this late in the season, especially with all the commotion I'm creating with rocks in the river.

As I throw my line back in the river, it hits me that the avalanche on the mountain was caused by me. I was thinking about whether I could send the rocks crashing down on Bobcat Mask, and I was concentrating on the gigantic boulder that was perched on the edge, waiting to fall. Now I'm sure, I made that boulder fall with the power of my thoughts. As I pull another fish to the riverbank I consider whether I should tell my companions about this strange ability that I have discovered. I knock the fish on the head with my new war club and remove its guts, then I clean it and return to our clearing. I cut cross sections of trout and set them on the rocks around the fire to dry for the winter.

Half an hour later, the healers return with baskets full of things that Gathers Seeds claims are edible. Clumps of all sorts of plants are tied to dry in the branches that hang around the clearing. I hope he can keep straight which ones are for medicinal purposes and which ones are for the cook pot.

I sit by the fire sculpting my war club as the day darkens from dusk to black. The darker it gets, the more I worry. Ferocious Wind is overdue. I have a horrible feeling that something has happened to her.

It's a sleepless night full of worry.

Chapter 19

I toss and turn all night and finally rise before dawn to start the day. Ferocious Wind still isn't home. This can't be good. I am sure that something terrible has happened to her, though in the past she has always seemed immortal. I try to force thoughts about what I would do without her from my mind, but they keep coming back to me. A sense of doom overwhelms me again. I move toward the fire to bring it back to life.

A loud voice bellows from the woods. "You are surrounded."

I drop back to the ground and look around for weapons. The healers have awakened. Their lifted heads wait for the voice to speak again.

The thunderous voice rings out. "Give up the White Warrior and we will let the rest of you go. Warrior Woman is dead. She can't save you."

The words hit me like a punch. Ferocious Wind is dead. I repeat it over and over, and each time it feels like another punch. Tears roll down my cheeks and I cover my face with my shaking hands, sobbing as silently as I can. The wild woman who was to be my mine is gone. I curl into a ball. I can hear the healers whispering, but I can't hear what they are saying. Our situation is hopeless anyway. I don't care what happens to me. I just want to melt into the soil and disappear forever. I wish I'd never met these people who are so bent on destroying each other. I wish the healers hadn't followed Ferocious

Wind and I wish they had not saved me. What good are wishes anyway? I shiver and wish desperately that I could be alone for a while.

The healers slide closer to me on their elbows. We argue in quiet voices. Three Fingers thinks that we should surrender together. Gathers Seeds disagrees. My mind is made up. "I must save you. There is no other way."

The voice in the woods hollers again. "Cross your arms over your chest and come out now, or we are coming in."

Three Fingers shouts. "He is not a warrior. He is a gentle soul. A captive. You must be mistaken. This is not the man you seek. Your fight is with Spits Teeth, not Conchobar."

Bobcat Mask doesn't acknowledge any of what Three Fingers has said. After a long arduous trip of tracking me, I'm sure that he is determined not to come away empty-handed. I can hear the impatience in his voice as he loudly commands, "Send him out now, or you all die. You decide." I'm deeply fearful. I must surrender and save the healers.

I rise to my feet and limp from the clearing, my head hanging low, my arms crossed over my chest. The feeling of doom that had been following me seems to have caught up with me.

The man at Bobcat Mask's side gasps, "That's the boy we found on the riverside near the ocean, remember? He's no warrior. He's just a child."

I look up long enough to glare at him. *I am no child.* Momentarily, I feel drawn toward the hatred for these people that Spits Teeth espouses. I bite my tongue. I am in no position to argue. I have surrendered to Bobcat Mask, and I have surrendered to fate. I am surprised to see that my captors are a party of three. In my vision, there were six men in the war party. I look around for the rest of them and I don't see anybody else.

My hands are tied tightly in front of me, and my ankles are tied loosely.

Bobcat Mask's voice roars out from behind the cat whiskers that dance in the breeze. "March!"

I hobble slowly down the path, and Bobcat Mask is frustrated by my slow pace. "Stop!" He cuts the cord that binds my ankles, then he orders me to march again.

All day, we march silently and we stop at dusk. I wonder where the other two men are and what will happen next. I have no power over the situation anyhow. Fully aware that the chief can do as he wishes, I promise myself that I will accept my fate and meet it as silently as possible. My only consolation is that my surrender has saved the healers, yet I worry about the missing members of Bobcat Mask's war party. And I think of Ferocious Wind.

The chief ties my ankles and binds them to my hands, then he shoves my shoulder and sends me flying to the ground. I land in a fetal position. He laughs as I hit the ground with a thud. Then he builds a fire with materials from a pack on his back.

An hour later, Three Fingers and Gathers Seeds are marched into the chief's camp by his son and the third warrior. I shout, "What are they doing here? You promised you'd let them go free if I surrendered."

The chief's son answers me. "We lied."

Bobcat Mask laughs. Then he spreads his blankets on the ground by the fire and promptly goes to sleep.

The autumn air is cold, cold enough that we could freeze to death. Gathers Seeds, Three Fingers and I wiggle close to one another to share body heat. We are forced to shiver through the cold night with no blankets. To make matters worse, I think of all that I have endured only to find myself a captive again. Rage overwhelms me. I feel ashamed that the curse that surrounds me has enveloped the healers as well. Now that she is gone, I have come to think of Ferocious Wind as my wife, and I wish she hadn't followed me. I should have sent her home, but I was too weak to think of what was best for her.

There's no denying that I'm cursed. Only the monks at the monastery and the puffins on the island were strong enough to survive me. It feels like I'm destined to careen from one tragedy to the next. I should never have taken that fishing boat. I think it was the one time I've done something reckless. I don't remember doing things that were forbidden by the monks, except for borrowing the boat without permission. If it weren't for that, I'd probably still be chopping stone at Skellig Michael, swinging the scythe and gathering thatch for our roofs, or hoeing the meager garden on the side of the island's mountain. The existence I once thought of as dull and dreary now seems glorious in retrospect. I close my eyes and I imagine that I can fly like a peregrine falcon around the tall peak that stands on the tiny island across the ocean. I miss the quiet, studious little men in their robes and wonder if Lector Beccán mourns me.

I imagine standing near the top of the peak and jumping out as far as possible, headfirst into the rocks below. It would be a painless and final end to the curse that follows me wherever I go. Maybe I can goad my captors into ending me before dragging me back to their village. The full extent of the idea burns through my chest. Though my life serves no purpose, it is still startling to think of it coming to an end.

In the morning as they're preparing for another exhausting day of marching, I can't help but ask about Ferocious Wind. I don't want to know, yet I can't help myself. I demand that they tell me what happened to her.

Bobcat Mask's son, Big Stoat, likes to talk. "She ambushed us, and I shot an arrow into her. She died like a warrior, without a whimper, and without a complaint. Too bad she killed three of our men."

The warrior next to Big Stoat shoves him. "Hush, you fool."

I know enough about these people to realize that Ferocious Wind's story will become legend. It will be told for generations in her home village and in the village of her enemy. As a warrior, she wouldn't have wanted anything more. I can empathize with most emotions, but I can't relate to the warrior's ethos, the glory of battle, the determination to vanquish enemies, and the lust for victory. I have trouble relating to those emotions. I think of the time I spent with Ferocious Wind and her death feels tragic, not glorious. I feel like the wind has been knocked out of me, like I am gasping for breath. The future we should have had together is gone.

I realize once I start talking that I must continue my plan until something happens. The words I plan to say cannot be taken back. I shudder, take a deep breath, and pitch my shoulders forward. I remember thinking about diving headfirst from the top of Skellig Michael. Enough thinking. It is time to act. I am no longer the obedient child of Lector Beccán.

"How many of your people did we kill when we attacked your village?" I can see my taunt has angered all three of our captors, not just Big Stoat.

Bobcat Mask barks a command, ordering me to be silent.

"And how many from Spits Teeth's village did you kill?" I feel like I can see steam coming from their ears. "Did you kill any of Spits Teeth's people? I'm guessing not. One day soon, Spits Teeth will finish you all off. Then he'll rip off that childish cat mask and piss on your ugly face. Again."

In a rage, Bobcat Mask storms over to me. I close my eyes and imagine a hatchet splitting my brains. I smile radiantly, tip my head back, push my chest forward and wait. "End me, piss face."

He shoves me to the ground and kicks me in the stomach. I writhe on the ground like a snake chopped in half, gasping for breath.

Bobcat Mask barks, "Get to your feet and march."

Big Stoat grabs my tied arms and lifts me back to a standing position. "No. I will not march. I will go no further. This is it for me." Then I command the angry chief again. "End me, piss face." I close my eyes and wait for a warclub to pound my skull. Instead, a swift high kick lands in the middle of my chest and I go flying backward.

I'm dragged to my feet once more. I taunt, "Take off that idiotic mask and let us see that hideous face of yours." This time, I'm sure the chief will quickly dispatch me himself. Rather, he swings his fist from behind him into my cheek with maximum force, hitting my jaw and sending me flying.

I stand stubbornly. My jaw hurts. I look into the chief's eyes, the human eyes that peer out from beneath the mask. I have no more insults. I just stand in front of him, silently, staring directly into his eyes. Finally, he tells me, "I don't care if we have to carry your broken body all the way home. Our whole village will enjoy torturing you until you cry, like the baby you are, and you beg for mercy. No matter how you plead, nothing will save you. So it is up to you. You can march, or we'll carry you. You're not that heavy anyway."

I stand stubbornly in front of him. "I am not your enemy. Spits Teeth is your enemy. You can do what you want to me. Set these other men free and I shall march. Otherwise, you can carry me. It's a long trip. I bet I'll get heavier with each passing hour."

Big Stoat and the other warrior look at each other. They know that Bobcat Mask will not be carrying me; that task will fall upon them. Then they look at their war chief. Will he let the healers go?

The chief barks at them. "Carry him."

Big Stoat throws me over his shoulder like he might carry a deer carcass. Before he can get very far, I writhe from his shoulders and drop to the ground. No matter how he tries to carry me, I wriggle free. I realize that I'm beginning to enjoy being disobedient. Big Stoat scowls at me when he has to stop and lift me back over his shoulders. He slaps my face in an attempt to teach me a lesson and yells at me to be still. I am enjoying his frustration. I goad him further. "Just drag your knife across my throat. Then I will be a lot easier to carry."

I can tell that he is considering it.

"Sure, your father will be angry, but he will get over it. Maybe you can tell him to carry me himself."

The more I think about Bobcat Mask's promise to torture and kill me in their village, the more determined I am that they should kill me now.

Angrily, Bobcat Mask stomps over and tells his men to get some poles and tie them together. Then they can tie me to the poles and carry me with the poles resting on their shoulders. I frown in defeat. My desperate suicide mission has ended in despair. I lie on my back, tied to a stretcher staring up into an ugly gray sky, unable to move. Something has been shoved in my mouth. My captors have grown tired of listening to my taunts. There's nothing more I can do. Today.

Chapter 20

Every time they remove the gag from my mouth, I recommence my insults. I don't know how I do it. It is so unlike me. I've spent a lifetime following orders, doing what I'm told, and being quiet. Having decided to end it all, it's hard to find myself marching toward a grisly death. I'm well aware of the torture that awaits. Between what I've witnessed and what I've been told, I remain determined to escape that fate. Yet what can I do? There's a long way yet to travel. I'll have to think of something.

Finally the day comes to an end and our captors quickly set up camp. They're tired and they fall asleep fast. I'm left on the ground, tied to the poles, facing up. Trying to sleep while gagged dries my mouth and makes me feel like I could suffocate. I begin to question the wisdom of taunting our captors.

Three Fingers and Gathers Seeds are able to wiggle their way to my side. We huddle together in the cold.

Three Fingers quietly tries to reassure us. "Somehow this will all work out. We should pray together to the Great Spirit for guidance, strength, and assistance." I'm not sure I agree with Three Fingers's optimism regarding the Great Spirit.

Gathers Seeds hisses through his teeth. "We never should have left the village." I've never seen Gathers Seeds angry before. Even given our predicament, I'm surprised by his change of demeanor, but

I can't begrudge him the right to be mad. "I never should have let you talk me into this."

Surprisingly, I realize that my right hand is next to Three Fingers's tied wrists. I explore the knots at his wrists with my fingers and I find they're loose. It takes some time, but I think I can free his hands. I hear Three Fingers quietly tell Gathers Seeds that I am untying the knots at his wrists. Three Fingers is in a position where he can see his wrists.

Gathers Seeds steams silently and tears stream down his cheeks. I wouldn't blame them if they both regretted the decision to follow me. I wish I could spit the gag from my mouth so that I could apologize to the healers. They never should have ended up in such a situation as this. I feel the knots giving way at the tip of my fingers.

Three Fingers says, "You're almost there, Conchobar. Tonight we shall escape. Whatever the outcome, it is worth taking this chance. Don't you agree, Gathers Seeds?" His partner nods agreement and looks into the darkness. I am aware that he doesn't wish to make eye contact.

The last segment of the knot at Three Fingers's wrists comes free. He sits up, peeks across the fire to where our captors sleep, and reaches across my body to free his partner. Then they untie my wrists. Untying me from the poles takes a long time.

Finally, we are free. We tiptoe beyond the light of the fire into the darkness, not knowing what lies ahead. When we reach a safe distance, we try to decide what to do next. It's cold and dark. We have nothing, no food, no water, nothing to keep us warm, and no weapons to protect us. Should we head south? How could we outrun our enemy by heading south in the sad condition that we're in? Should we head back to the north? That's exactly what our enemy would expect. That leaves east or west.

I have a suggestion. "How about you head east. Then when you feel safe, return to our encampment to the north. If I survive, I'll meet you there."

Three Fingers asks what I mean when I say, "If I survive."

"When you are a safe distance away, I could sneak back into the camp, steal their weapons, kill Bobcat Mask and take the others as my prisoners. Or, I could just steal their weapons. I just need to make sure that I don't wake them accidentally, and I must pray that they don't wake up unexpectedly."

Gathers Seeds shakes his head, his chin at his chest. At this point, I don't think he'd agree with anything I suggest.

Three Fingers sputters. "I don't know what we should do. We are not warriors. Our purpose is to heal people, not kill them."

I am flooded with remorse. "I never imagined that I would kill or harm another human being. I'm a simple mason. I'm a builder, not a destroyer. After I was forced to attack the sleeping village, I vowed never to harm anyone again. But Bobcat Mask must be stopped. Maybe it isn't my job to stop him, but if he survives, you know what will happen to me."

Three Fingers's deep comforting voice tries to reassure me. He says he knows that I will do what I am supposed to do in a manner that would have me believe that the Great Spirit wishes for my success. "We shall pray for you." Gathers Seeds says nothing.

The healers tiptoe into the darkness and are gone. I'm totally alone. I don't even feel like myself anymore as I tiptoe back toward the fire that warms the enemy.

I'm so tempted to tiptoe past their fire and head into the woods. I would love to disappear into the wild western forest. It's a perfect plan. They'll never expect me to go in that direction. I'm not a fighter. I'm not a warrior. I've learned to survive in the wild. It won't be easy. I'll be free of both villages. Let them destroy each other if that's what they're destined to do. Their struggles never were my concern. I just had the misfortune to wash ashore at the wrong moment. Even if they manage to recapture Three Fingers and Gathers Seeds, I'm sure they'll let them go. What purpose would it serve to harm them?

I'm standing twenty feet from the circle of light that surrounds the fire and the sleeping war party. I have a huge decision to make, and no time to dither. I must decide quickly. I take a few steps toward the west, then stop. When will there ever be a better opportunity to dispatch Bobcat Mask? If he were dead, perhaps the warring villages could find peace. How many lives could be saved? I am but one and they are three. Should I protect myself or try to save these people. One village wants to kill me. The other village has banished me. The woman I love is dead. I don't owe anyone anything, except for the shivering healers who have done so much to help me.

I realize that I've made another decision that defies logic and goes against everything I believe in. It is a decision that I am certain will lead to my death. I guess I've always expected that I will die young. I know that life is precious, even lives that are hard to live. Perhaps Ferocious Wind watches over me from the other side. Though the night is cold, I feel sweat on my palms. My muscles are tense and I'm panting like a wild animal. My mouth is dry. I feel an urge to flee but the instinct to fight is greater. Tonight, I will fight.

The short walk back into camp seems to take all night. I'm careful not to drag my twisted ankle. At each step, I'm afraid that the enemy will awaken. At last, I'm standing by the fire. I see an abandoned knife by the fire and a hatchet a short distance away. With any luck, I won't need more than the knife.

I look at the farthest man. I shouldn't be surprised to see that he sleeps in the mask. Then I look to his sleeping son, eight feet away, curled up in a ball. The third warrior is stretched out on his back on the ground, his long neck fully exposed. Doubt creeps back into my mind. I shake my shoulders. I have decided. I can't listen to doubt. I must act. Simultaneously, I cover the third warrior's mouth and drag the abandoned knife across his throat. His body thrashes briefly, then he is gone.

Big Stoat has shifted in his sleep. I can feel my face, red hot in the cold night air, and I can smell the blood of the dead man by the fire. Big Stoat has a short, thick neck. I think I can position my knife for a quick strike. I pray that my luck will hold. I tiptoe to Big Stoat's side. In order to have the best chance, I'm forced to turn my back on Bobcat Mask. I drop to a squatting position and my knees crack. I reach forward with my knife, adrenaline coursing through my gut. Instead of cutting the man's throat, I find myself flying across his body. I twist slightly, my shoulder slams into the ground, and the knife slices a gash across my thigh, just above my knee.

I start to roll, attempt to jump to my feet, and try to recall if there are any weapons within reach. I don't even have a chance to leave the ground. Bobcat Mask jumps onto me, pinning me to the ground with his hand on my forehead. It is impossible for me to move. Big Stoat sleepily rises from his blankets, rubs his eyes, and asks what happened. I can barely see him in my peripheral vision.

Bobcat Mask ignores his son. Somehow I can tell that his jaws are clenched even behind the mask. "You have no idea how much I want to kill you. Right here. Right now. I know it will be so much more rewarding to watch the women and children peel your skin from your body and kill you slowly. Maybe they'll remove your fingers and toes first. The last sound you'll hear in this world will be my laughter." As if to ensure that I will know it when I hear it, Bobcat Mask tips his head back and laughs loudly, as if he were trying to call the wolves to camp.

Big Stoat has figured out what has happened, and hurries to tie me up. There's no chance of escaping now. I'm hardly able to move. They ask me where the healers are. I tell them that I don't know. "They ran off into the night hours ago." Incredibly, Bobcat Mask and Big Stoat go back to sleep. I lie awake, wishing for sleep.

In the morning, I'm left with Big Stoat while Bobcat Mask goes to round up the healers. I wish for a way to warn them and I pray that they are able to escape. I worry that the expert woodsman will easily track the healers.

Big Stoat is angry about the loss of his friend. As he fashions a travois to carry his fallen comrade home, he growls at me and makes a choking motion with his hands. I understand what he'd like to do to me. I offer apologies and try to find some way to establish a rapport. I know what they have planned for me. It's all I can think about. Perhaps I can learn something from him that will be useful to know. "What became of Warrior Woman? What did you do with her body?"

He answers with a sneer. "We pitched her dead body over the edge of a cliff and watched it bounce off the rocks below. The ravens were on her before she hit the ground."

I'm sure that he is exaggerating for effect. It works. It is hard to imagine the body of the woman you love being pecked apart by ravenous birds.

"How did she kill three warriors?" My question goes unanswered. I ask dozens of more questions, every question I can think to ask. Big Stoat ignores my inquiries and is as silent as the monks at Skellig Michael. Eventually I give up, lie down, and fall asleep.

At dusk, Big Stoat wakes me with a foot in my side. The healers are approaching the camp, followed by Bobcat Mask. Three Fingers's body is scratched up. It looks like he rolled down a hillside covered with thorny bushes. Gathers Seeds's lips are pinched tightly together and his eyes appear to be looking at the tip of his nose.

Chapter 21

In the morning, Bobcat Mask barks orders, eager to get started down the trail. Big Stoat doesn't move fast enough, and Bobcat Mask orders us to help get ready to march.

I resume my insolent strategy and tell the chief that I refuse to help and I refuse to march. He opens his mouth, and I'm expecting a fury. It comes from Gathers Seeds instead. He has had enough. He screams and runs straight at me. Bobcat Mask might think that Gathers Seeds is charging at him. It happens so fast. The war chief swings his arm and smashes the healer's head with his club. Gathers Seeds crumples to the ground at my feet and Bobcat Mask stomps off in a fury.

Three Fingers runs to his partner's side. From a kneeling position, he pulls Gathers Seeds's head and shoulders onto his lap. Gathers Seeds moans and blood spills from his lips onto Three Fingers's legs. Three Fingers closes his eyes. The sight of his grieving hits me like a punch in the stomach. Three Fingers rocks slowly and hums, tears streaming down his face as his partner draws his last breath. My damned curse has claimed another innocent life.

Moments later, Bobcat Mask stomps back over, yanks Gathers Seeds's body away from Three Fingers and throws it into the fire. Then he tells me that if I utter so much as a word, Three Fingers will be killed next. That threat ensures my obedience and compliance.

Poor Three Fingers must leave his partner, burning in an open grave. His head tilts downward and his hand covers his mouth. Two long, bony fingers stretch across his cheek. He turns away and heads southward down the trail. I've never seen someone look so defeated.

I wish there was something I could say to console my friend who marches silently at my side. He should hate me, blame me, and want me dead. I would probably feel that way if I were him. I know that I caused Gathers Seeds's death. The two men were so close, it is hard to imagine one without the other. Having grown up with men who spent most of their time in silence, I'm usually comfortable with silence myself. Today, being silent is breaking my heart.

The other thought that occupies my mind as we march endlessly through the woods is to look for an opportunity to jump from the trail to my death. What better way to end my life and join my beloved in the world of spirits than to bounce from rock to rock as she did? Let the damned carrion birds pick my bones clean. It is better than being skinned alive in Bobcat Mask's village.

As the day goes on, Three Fingers moves slower and slower. Maybe it is the grief. Maybe it is sleeplessness. Perhaps he is sick. There are still hours of marching before dusk. His legs buckle and his tall, thin body crumbles to the ground. I hurry to help him back to his feet. He tells me that he must have fallen asleep. I nod to indicate that I have heard him. I know that I mustn't speak. Instead, I concentrate and think of what I would like to say to this man.

His eyes grow wide and he looks directly at me. I forgot that we can communicate without words, and Three Fingers must have forgotten too. His gaze seems to drill through my eyes and into my brain. I can hear his thoughts. I can feel his pain. There is no blame. Somehow he doesn't think that it is my fault. If it weren't for me, he could not endure his life without Gathers Seeds. He knows my heart. His soul knows my soul from a distant time and a faraway place. There is something we are meant to do together. We shall figure out what that is. Soon. Now we must march.

Our shared thoughts last for a matter of seconds. I have a sense of elation. It is as if the curse has lifted and been replaced by magic. We are still prisoners. Angry people with weapons are steps away from us, but I feel transformed by the power of optimism. Walking beside Three Fingers, I reflect optimism back to him. When he slows down, I cheer him on. When I feel him starting to stumble, I jump to his side and prevent him from falling.

Late in the afternoon, we startle a deer. Bobcat Mask has his bow in his hand and brings the deer to the ground with an arrow. It is good that we are making camp early. Three Fingers needs to rest. Our captors understand that we need food to be strong enough to march. We are untied briefly and allowed to eat until we're unable to eat any longer. It's good to have a full belly. In the morning, Three Fingers is stronger. He marches at a steady pace and doesn't fall.

How strange to converse using only our thoughts. It seems invasive on the one hand, and a wonderful gift on the other. There aren't many people I would trust with free access to my every thought. In this moment, it is a most convenient skill to possess.

Big Stoat leads the way, dragging the travois that carries the man I killed in their camp. I don't know why his eyes are open. Perhaps Bobcat Mask's people don't close the eyes of the dead. The dead man's eyes popped open just as I was slicing his neck. Now his wide eyes watch me follow him through the woods. I imagine him cursing me from beyond. I wonder about his family and I feel guilty for ending his life. Three Fingers's thoughts enter my mind like roots stretching deeper into the soil. *Don't blame yourself. It couldn't be helped. He would do the same to you. That's how* we *are.*

But what if it didn't have to be that way?

What do you mean?

What if we could find a way for the people of Spits Teeth's village and the people of Bobcat Mask's village to stop killing each other endlessly. What if there were a way to bring them together and cause a lasting peace. If we don't, they'll destroy each other. They're well on their way to doing that already.

Three Fingers scratches his chin in thought. *Yes, there must be a way. But how?*

What if there were a way to get Spits Teeth and Bobcat Mask to fight each other. One-on-one. Man-to-man. Wouldn't that be better than village versus village? What if the parties promised that the villages would know peace after that? Do you think that their hatred really extends beyond their hatred for one another?

He turns and twists his face at me in a way that makes me think he's not so sure. *Almost all of our people's stories are legends of battles between the villages. It doesn't mean that it could not happen. I think we'd find an ally in Hole in the Roof. Even if it doesn't result in peace between the villages, it might just save you.*

I nod. It is a stretch. *Maybe you could suggest it to Bobcat Mask. You could tell him that people will tell his story over and over, forever. All he has to do is defeat Spits Teeth. Appeal to his ego. Tell him that he has always known that he could defeat this enemy, and that he really should have done so a long time ago. Tell him that nobody in Spits Teeth's village likes him anyway. He'd be doing both villages a favor.*

What would we tell Spits Teeth?

I smile at Three Fingers. *Almost exactly the same thing.*

Three Fingers worries. *What if Bobcat Mask isn't convinced? What if Spits Teeth doesn't accept the invitation?*

You could tell him that if Spits Teeth doesn't accept, that you will leave his village and move to Bobcat Mask's village. I'm sure they could use a powerful healer and seer.

I can tell that Three Fingers is thinking about it. *Now, how do we save you?*

Well, you can tell him that I was banished. Spits Teeth hates me, and it will anger Spits Teeth if Bobcat Mask keeps me alive. You can tell him that Spits Teeth blames me for killing most of his family. That's probably true anyhow. Of course, you can tell Bobcat Mask that he can still torture and kill me if Spits Teeth refuses to come.

Three Fingers nods. *What if Spits Teeth accepts the invitation, but loses? What then?*

I shrug. *Perhaps they'll forget about me. They'll be so busy celebrating that I can disappear like I'm not there. Maybe the two villages will become one village, or maybe they'll become motivated to live in peace. You could step forward as a seer and tell them that the Great Spirit wishes for them to have peace instead of war.*

But it's true. I know it is. If I could have found a way to bring peace to the villages I would have done it a long time ago. It is a good plan. We have everything to gain. Let's consider what could go wrong.

That's always been hard for me. The world is full of danger. Bad things happen all the time and yet I'm always surprised when they do. We discuss all the awful things that could happen, mind-to-mind as we walk, mile after mile. *What if the villages break out in violence during the one-on-one battle between the war chiefs? What if Spits Teeth wins and banishes me again? What if the winning chief attacks the village of the other? Would the other village be powerless to defend itself without a war chief? What about the councils, do they need to approve? Will they agree?*

After contemplating every downside we can imagine, we agree that it seems like a good idea.

After we set up camp for the night, I listen as Three Fingers softly asks Bobcat Mask for a few words. Fortunately, his request is granted. "You may not know this. I am not just a healer but a seer also. Sometimes I have powerful visions. Today, my vision comes with a suggestion. See if you can picture it too. You invite Spits Teeth to a battle—a battle to the death. In my vision, you are standing on his chest, waving his scalp in your hand. When you defeat him, you will declare peace between our villages. The Great Spirit wishes for peace now. You will become a legend and your story will be told for generations to come. You are powerful and my vision is strong. Perhaps when we arrive in your village, you can send me to Spits Teeth's village. I will not tell him about my vision. You must keep the White Warrior alive. Spits Teeth hates him, and I will need to offer him to Spits Teeth as a prize in case he wins the battle. Of course, he won't win, but we need to get him to accept your invitation."

I feel like I can see the delight on his face. Clearly, Bobcat Mask loves the idea. It is as if the facial expressions beneath the mask carry forward onto the face of the bobcat skin. For the rest of our journey, Bobcat Mask is jubilant. It feels like he is celebrating his victory, though the battle hasn't been confirmed yet. His son looks at him like he has gone mad.

Chapter 22

The war chief returns to his village a hero, as if being the chief isn't prestigious enough.

Three Fingers and I are tied to a pole on an elevated platform, placed on display for all to see. Bobcat Mask tells the story of how they battled Warrior Woman. Big Stoat puffs out his chest and nods as Bobcat Mask tells the story of our capture. I look at Three Fingers as they overstate the difficulty of capturing us. Then Bobcat Mask tells the gathered crowd about the plan to challenge Spits Teeth as if it were his own idea. "We must see to the safety of the White Warrior. He's our bait. When I've destroyed Spits Teeth, you can have him." Bobcat Mask points to an angry-looking woman standing a few feet in front of him. The teenaged boys standing next to her look at me with hatred in their eyes. I'm sure they are the family of the warrior that accompanied Big Stoat and Bobcat Mask. I look out over the crowd. They're all staring at me as if I am the devil himself.

Bobcat Mask tells his son to take us to his longhouse and make sure that we're tied up securely. Then he heads off with a dozen villagers. I ask Big Stoat what is happening. "They talk, then think, then vote." Clearly, my fate lies in the hands of others.

As the crowd dissipates, we are left standing on the platform. I turn my head and look off into the distance. I see the tree up on the hill, the tree that we climbed to spy upon Bobcat Mask's village. Only the last of its leaves remain on its branches, stubbornly clinging to a season that has passed. The image of the tree reminds me of something I can't place. It speaks to me, but for some reason, I'm oblivious to the message I am supposed to receive. Three Fingers clears his throat to get my attention. Big Stoat is waiting. It is time for us to move. I glance back at the tree on the hill and frown.

As we walk by, the angry woman spits a giant glob of phlegm at me and it lands on my chin. Everyone else tries to touch me. I cringe, trying to shrink within myself, wishing they would leave me alone and wondering what the big deal is. Certainly, this village has dealt with enemy captives before. Then I remember that they've never seen anybody that looks like me.

Finally, we make it to Bobcat Mask's longhouse. I can't help but look around. It is startling how similar this building is to the building that Spits Teeth lives in. Everything about the village seems almost identical. I can't help but think that their hating each other is a form of hating themselves.

The hours pass slowly as we sit quietly by the fire in the chief's compartment. I memorize the surroundings, making a mental note of where everything is. I recall the story that Three Fingers told of Spits Teeth's captivity. I try to picture a young version of Spits Teeth sleeping on the floor, bound and tied to the frame of the chief's bunk. Then I recall the part of the story in which Spits Teeth escapes and mutilates Bobcat Mask's face, tattooing that image on his cheek.

Hours later, Bobcat Mask returns from the council meeting. "They want to speak with the captive." I rise to my feet, prepared to follow the chief. He roughly pushes me back to the floor. "Not you." He points to Three Fingers and leads him away. I'm left wondering what this strange development means. *Is it good news, somehow?*

The council takes so long to decide what to do, I can't help falling asleep in a heap on the dirt floor of the longhouse. In the morning, I awaken before everyone else. I look around in the dim light, my eyes adjusting slowly. I can see Bobcat Mask sleeping, ten feet away. Perhaps it is the air escaping from his nose beneath, but it looks like the whiskers on his mask are twitching. I feel a rush of fear in my gut as I remember that my fate remains uncertain. I look around for Three Fingers, and I can't see him. I have no choice but to lie here quietly, waiting for people to wake up.

Finally, Bobcat Mask wakes up, looks at me, immobilized beside the fire, asks me if I am enjoying his hospitality. Instead of answering, I ask him where Three Fingers is. He shrugs, tells me that they killed him at council, and turns toward the exit. Before disappearing into the morning, he turns and tells me that I will be next, perhaps in a day or two, maybe three if I'm lucky.

I had known that this was a possible outcome. I was so sure that our clever plan would prevent this. It seemed that Bobcat Mask loved the idea of defeating his enemy in hand-to-hand combat. I know nothing of the rest of Bobcat Mask's people. I am surprised that the council members didn't accept the plan. It's hard to believe that Three Fingers is gone now too.

Most of the time I feel like a man, but I can't help feeling like a child as I think about the certainty of my impending demise. I wonder why tears don't flood my eyes now that Three Fingers has been killed. Maybe I'm too angry to be sad. Bobcat Mask told me that it is coming. He didn't say when. I wonder if it would be easier to know, rather than to think that each time someone enters the longhouse or approaches the fire, they are coming to get me. To take me away. To lead me to the platform in the center of the village. I don't know if I can maintain honor and dignity when they do all the horrible things to me that Bobcat Mask promised.

I'm fed, offered water, and led to the open pit latrine only when Big Stoat remembers that he's responsible for keeping me alive so that I can be killed when it's convenient, or when it serves the entertainment needs of the village. When I am taken outside, my eyes are always drawn up the hill to the globed shape of the maple tree. It seems to call to me and I wonder what to make of it.

On the third day of waiting to die a horrible death, I mournfully think of Three Fingers. I'm surprised to hear his voice when I think of him. *We shall arrive in the village shortly.*

I reply in my thoughts, *Whatever do you mean? Are you a spirit? I was told you were killed.*

No, they sent me to bring Spits Teeth as we planned. Did they tell you otherwise?

Yes, Bobcat Mask told me that you were killed at council and that I would be the next to die. Only, nobody speaks to me or looks at me, with the brief exception of Big Stoat. Must be he wanted me to suffer with worry. I'm so glad you're alive and that Spits Teeth is on his way. When will you arrive?

Within the hour. Say your prayers.

Just a little bit of hope makes me feel so much better. Perhaps our plans will work. Maybe I will survive. I hope to lead a tranquil life among a small group of people and work at creating lasting beauty and order from stone. Such a humble dream should be possible to achieve, yet it seems like a distant, unlikely possibility.

An hour later, I hear a commotion outside the longhouse. I feel a combination of excitement and worry. Through the walls, I hear Three Fingers tell Bobcat Mask that they must first release the White Warrior. Spits Teeth will arrive in camp when the sun peaks in the sky. Bobcat Mask growls at his son. "Send the captive out."

I feel excited. It seems like ages since I have had the freedom to move my limbs, unobstructed. The simple act of being able to scratch an itch, or shoo a fly, feels like a luxury. I'm surprised when I walk through the doorway of the longhouse and see Three Fingers and a dozen people surrounding him, including Hole in the Roof and Dancing Bear. Standing to Three Fingers's left is Tends Hearth. She's wearing a beautifully decorated buckskin dress, and her head is tilted down, but I can see that her eyes are watching me.

This woman who hates me, calls me cursed, and had me banished, why is she here?

Three Fingers has heard my thoughts, and his answer brings shockwaves to my mind. *Be prepared, my friend. It turns out that she doesn't hate you. It's quite the opposite, in fact. Don't break her heart. She has been through a lot as well.*

I'm surprised to see the enemy extend hospitality to Spits Teeth's people. The women of Bobcat Mask's village bring them food and drink and make them comfortable at the perimeter of what is to be the battleground, right in the middle of their village. One by one, the villagers take up positions on the grass, sitting cross-legged as if they're waiting for a picnic lunch to be served. The people chatter, gossip, and laugh as if a battle to the death happens in the middle of their village every day.

For a brief moment, Tends Hearth and I are alone within a crowd. She looks up at me tentatively. "I'm so sorry. I was just awful to you. I was jealous and mean, and every time I tried to say I loved you I said something horrible instead. I don't know what came over me. Don't hate me. Please, please, please tell me that you can forgive me. I'll never be mean to you again. Whether you're cursed or not, I don't care anymore." Her gaze drops away from me and she is quiet. I suppose she's waiting for me to say something.

I put my hand on her shoulder and tell her not to worry, I don't hate her, and I understand. A vision floods my mind. I remember the awe-inspiring image of the tree on her back, a result of the lightning strike that she survived. That is what came to mind when I was looking at the big maple tree on the hill. Was it a premonition of sorts? But a premonition of what?

Three Fingers is looking at me like I imagine a proud mother might look at her son. *I think you'll find she's very sweet, if you just give her a chance. Pretty girl.*

I reach for Tends Hearth's hand and take it in mine. Her touch is electric. It is as if she has saved the power of the lightning and is now releasing it through her hand. I'm reminded of my spirit's trip through the roots of trees beneath the earth and passing from tree to tree. I look up from our joined hands into Tends Hearth's eyes and she smiles shyly. It's as though we are totally alone until all at once, the noisy crowd is silent. I look up to the platform. There stands Spits Teeth. I drop his daughter's hand. I imagine that he has come to kill me after banishing me from his village, only I know that he is here for Bobcat Mask.

I look at Tends Hearth. I wonder if she is worried. This young girl could lose her father today. "Are you going to be okay?"

"Yes, now that you're here."

I point to my chest in disbelief. She nods her head and bats her eyes.

Chapter 23

The crowd has gathered and has become a boisterous mob, despite the small number of people remaining in Bobcat Mask's village. The sight of the enemy war chief has roused their anger.

Spits Teeth is an impressive warrior. He's muscular and strong, despite his forty years. He's covered in red and black paint, small round dots in some places and thick lines in others. I know the designs mean something to him and perhaps to our people. He stands aggressively, legs and arms bent slightly. It is the same stance I remember Ferocious Wind assuming on numerous occasions. It looks like he could pounce in any direction or jump clear across the gathering grounds. He growls through clenched teeth.

Spits Teeth's challenge is answered by a high pitched cat call from the other side of the clearing. Bobcat Mask is an equally imposing figure. His body is painted blue and the frightening cat mask conveys its perpetual roar. He enters slowly, stomping the ground heavily with his feet. His people cheer him on as he pounds his chest. "I see you have accepted my invitation. This time you have come yourself rather than sending your daughter."

The angry men exchange a lifetime of insults, the audience from both villages know their history all too well. *You stole my childhood. You killed my family. You ruined what was supposed to be the best day of my life. You killed my sons.*

Tends Hearth covers her eyes and peeks between her fingers as Spits Teeth jumps from the platform and lands inches from Bobcat Mask. Dancing Bear and Big Stoat run toward the enemies and separate them. The combatants are stripped of all of their weapons except for their favorite knives. One end of a twelve-foot-long cord is tied to each man's right ankle. Dancing Bear and Big Stoat take turns checking the tightness of the knots.

As Dancing Bear returns to the side of our leader, Big Stoat holds a hand up, commanding silence from the crowd. He looks directly at me and points his finger in my direction. "As soon as Spits Teeth is dead I'm going to slice you open. I'll unravel your insides and tie them to that pole. We'll see how long you can last." The crowd roars with delight, as if they were hoping for such entertainment.

I want to crawl into a hole. I'm sure that I am going to vomit. I knew I had a vested interest in the outcome of this fight. I had hoped that my captors had forgotten me. I grimace as Tends Hearth's fingernails dig into my skin, but I'm grateful for the diversion.

Big Stoat turns back toward the combatants. In a loud voice he asks the crowd if they're ready. The air fills with their cheers. Big Stoat waits a few moments then raises his hand again. He loudly announces, "Let the battle begin."

Bobcat Mask starts by hollering, "Prepare to die."

Big Stoat turns back toward me and drags his thumb across his neck. If it weren't for Tends Hearth, I might attempt to flee.

Spits Teeth runs as fast as he can, directly into Bobcat Mask, and wallops him with such force that he bounces back from the impact. Bobcat Mask flies to the ground, his knife dragging along the surface of Spits Teeth's left shin. Instead of capitalizing on the opportunity to gut Bobcat Mask with his knife, Spits Teeth rips the mask from his adversary's face.

The crowd gasps at the hideous sight. Nobody in Bobcat Mask's village has seen his face since it was mutilated by Spits Teeth, all those years ago. The proud man roars like a wounded bear and jumps from the ground. The hatred on his face is even uglier than the horrible tattooing on his cheeks. Spits Teeth throws the mask toward the spectators. It lands at the feet of Hole in the Roof. She slowly bends her arthritic knees and lowers herself to the ground. She picks up the mask and holds it between her elbow and her side.

Bobcat Mask circles to his right and Spits Teeth matches his movement in the opposite direction. After ten steps, Spits Teeth feints left, jerks right, and rushes Bobcat Mask again. He surprises his host with a foot in his belly rather than attacking with his knife. Bobcat Mask crashes into the ground again and the crowd moans its disappointment.

Spits Teeth must win for *my* safety to be guaranteed. Tends Hearth leans into my side. It's as if she is trying to hide behind me. She's lost so many siblings. Now her father is engaged in a fight to the death. I remember all of my unpleasant encounters with the miserable, hardheaded, disagreeable man that banished me. Now I must pray for him to be victorious. Not just for my sake, but for his daughter's.

It's hard to keep track of the action when grown men are wrestling on the ground with knives. I look away briefly and see the spectators' heads leaning toward the fight, turning and twisting, one direction after another, trying to see what is happening. I glance at Hole in the Roof. She doesn't turn or twist her head. I wonder whether she can see that far away. Maybe it doesn't matter to her which way it goes. Perhaps she already knows the outcome.

Moments later, Bobcat Mask rushes Spits Teeth, who backs away quickly. They're headed toward the crowd and they're coming our way. At the last moment, Spits Teeth veers to our right, crashing directly into Hole in the Roof.

The crowd gives way. The deadly dance has moved back toward the center of the battlefield. Our matriarch looks like a corpse, limbs akimbo, knocked out on the ground. Dancing Bear and Three Fingers run to her side.

The crowd is divided. Who will win the battle? Will Hole in the Roof survive? Some watch the fight and some watch the healer and the medicine man tend to our leader.

The old enemies fight on for what seems like ages. Again, the old enemies have found their feet and stand across from each other. It is as if both are waiting for the other to move. Both look exhausted. I wonder whether they can feel the pain from the countless cuts on their bodies. It amazes me that neither one has landed a knife in a fat vein or a vital organ. I hate to admit it, but it looks like Bobcat Mask is stronger, and Spits Teeth's wounds look more substantial. A long gash across his forehead is bleeding profusely. Both men are panting from exertion and sweating like it's a hot summer's day rather than a cold day in autumn.

I cringe at the thought that this battle is almost over. I drape my arm around Tends Hearth's shoulders and she rests her head on my chest. We brace ourselves for the end.

I cast a quick glance toward Hole in the Roof. Dancing Bear and Three Fingers are helping her to her feet. She is stronger than she looks. From the expression on her face it doesn't appear that she is in pain—ever stoic. I grind my teeth and hope that I'll be able to face whatever is coming my way with similar composure, and shudder as I think about my insides being yanked from my stomach.

Back in the clearing, Bobcat Mask makes a quick movement, just a couple of inches forward. The fake sends Spits Teeth into a charge which Bobcat Mask sidesteps. Spits Teeth is moving so fast that he outruns the cord that binds his ankle and he crashes onto the ground with a sound that reminds me of the day that the falling tree killed Fern. On impact, Spits Teeth begins rolling. Bobcat Mask lands on top of him.

We see Bobcat Mask's right arm high in the air. The crowd howls. I brace myself. Bobcat Mask slams his knife deep into Spits Teeth's chest. Despite his hideously marred face, Bobcat Mask's face reflects the proud countenance of victory. Then it twists into itself and he collapses on top of his enemy.

Tends Hearth has turned her back to the battle, and her sobbing face is planted on my chest. I have one hand on her back and my other hand gently holds the back of her head. I can tell that she is having a hard time standing, knowing that her father has died. I'm watching intently over the top of her head, trying to figure out what is happening and what comes next. I attempt to reassure her that she will be alright. Then I hum the song that Three Fingers used to hum to soothe me, when I arrived in their village. I hope that the sound of my voice is helping Tends Hearth focus on something other than her grief. It's not doing much for me as I shiver in fear. Big Stoat's threat weighs heavy on my mind.

The crowd is silent. Except for glances at one another, and my muted bombinating, nobody makes a sound. Everyone can see that Spits Teeth is dead, but what about Bobcat Mask? Why isn't he moving?

Finally, Big Stoat rushes to his father's side and rolls him away from Spits Teeth. The handle of Spits Teeth's knife is planted deeply in Bobcat Mask's blood-drenched belly. The crowd lets out another deep collective moan. I stop humming and my mouth hangs open. I tell Tends Hearth that Bobcat Mask is dead. I am looking at both warriors lying dead on the ground, side by side, having suffered the same fate, the fate that they both deserve. I can't believe I never considered the possibility of this outcome. What now?

I'm surprised when Tends Hearth pulls away from me and runs to her father's side, still sobbing. She bends at the waist and turns toward the crowd, swinging her arms dramatically. "Let this be the end. We have been at war for so long, nobody even knows when it began, or why we hate each other. Instead of destroying each other, our people must become one. We must fight no more."

Everyone watches as Hole in the Roof slowly steps forward, walks across the gathering ground, and hands Big Stoat his father's mask. Then she offers her hands to Big Stoat. Her gesture gives us hope that there can be peace.

She is left standing in front of him with her empty hands rejected. He turns his back to her and runs straight at me, tackling me to the ground. He twists my neck and presses my face into the muddy ground. I hear a voice telling Big Stoat that his father promised that I would be released. He releases his grip on me and I roll away.

He stands and proclaims, "The White Warrior can leave over my dead body." I can't believe my ears. Big Stoat announces that I can walk away from their village if I can defeat him. The crowd cheers at the prospect of a second battle. Evidently I don't get a say in the matter. Minutes later the long rope binds our feet and we're facing each other, knives in hand. I haven't had time to consider a plan. I never anticipated this. Abruptly, Big Stoat has his head ducked like a bison and he's charging directly toward me. Should I dart to the left or the right? I have moments to decide and I don't know what to do, until a root catches his foot and he crashes into the dirt. I hear Ferocious Wind's voice in my ear, and the words from my warrior training. "In a battle, it's them or you. Life or death. If you fail, one of our comrades dies. A wife loses a husband. A family loses a provider. You must not hesitate. You must defeat them." I jump on his back and sink my knife into his heart. I twist the blade aggressively until Big Stoat is motionless beneath me.

As I stand I think of the curse. It should have been me that tripped. Perhaps the curse has been broken, somehow—and where did that root come from? There isn't a tree within hundreds of yards of the gathering grounds.

A wailing woman steps from the crowd and shouts at Hole in

the Roof, pointing at the palisade walls. "Go. Take Spits Teeth and the White Warrior and leave. Now." She turns and stomps off. The crowd in Bobcat Mask's village is left standing, wondering about their future. Nobody steps forward.

Tends Hearth and I offer our arms to Hole in the Roof. She accepts our assistance and we lead her toward the village's exit. She says, "Perhaps we shall have peace after they grieve. So few people remain in their village."

Chapter 24

Spits Teeth's village isn't sufficiently larger. With the loss of our war chief and an aging matriarch, it is hard to imagine who will lead our people. On the way home, Hole in the Roof asks Tends Hearth whether she would consider leading the Women's Council. The matriarch must have been impressed with Tends Hearth's speech in Bobcat Mask's village to make such a suggestion. Tends Hearth graciously declines.

The slow march home provides us with the time to plan our future together. I tell Tends Hearth that I plan to live alone in the wilderness, far to the north. I have accepted that I'm not meant to live in a large village. With her hand in mine, I ask if she would like to join me as my wife. She stops in the middle of the path and jumps into my arms. I can't help but smile so hard that it hurts. It would seem that she likes the idea. If someone had told me yesterday that this would happen, I would have been shocked by the mere suggestion.

My enthusiasm is dampened by the notion of the curse. I remind Tends Hearth of what she said about my being cursed. Then I tell her that my father cursed my mother, her child, and all who descend from me. Three Fingers is walking nearby. He usually isn't one to interrupt, but in this instance, he offers his opinion. Then he asks Dancing Bear to make a formal declaration.

That's one of Dancing Bear's favorite things to do. He stops our march briefly and gathers us together to make an announcement. He declares that I am not cursed and suggests that my banishment be rescinded. Hole in the Roof declares that I am not banished and invites me to stay in the village.

I'm grateful and overwhelmed. I thank them, apologize, and decline. Instead I ask if Tends Hearth and I can be married immediately. Hole in the Roof frowns. It is a rare expression of emotion for the stoic matriarch. Marriages are not permitted in our village while we are in mourning.

Three Fingers asks if the marriage could be held outside of the village. "The only problem is, who could grant the maiden permission to marry?" Three Fingers looks directly into Dancing Bear's eyes.

"Oh, I could. Yes, I could do that."

There's no time for second thoughts or contemplation. Twenty minutes later the ceremony is complete and we recommence our march toward home.

Our traveling party wishes us well as we walk. Everyone agrees that it is foolish to head north so late in the season. Despite their sage advice, I remain committed to an immediate departure. I have spent too long in captivity. I have a picture in my mind of the place I plan to live. Perhaps it's a premonition. One night back in Spits Teeth's longhouse is one night too many for me.

The hardest part is leaving Fish Basket and Loon Feather. I worry about how they will survive. Between them, only one child remains. How can Struts Like a Goose provide for them? I have never seen him do much more than gather kindling and turn wood into sawdust. I feel a sense of obligation to change my plan and provide for Tends Hearth's family. If only there were another way. I'm just about to give up on my plans for the future when Dancing Bear enters the longhouse and asks for Fish Basket and Loon Feather's hand in marriage. I turn to face the widows and they nod. Will wonders never cease?

Our next visitor is Three Fingers, who arrives just as Dancing Bear is leaving. He has come from the healer's lodge. "I can't live there without Gathers Seeds. That time has gone. I must move on. Could I move north with you?"

Enthusiastically, I tell him that I'm happy he will join us. It would be hard to leave him behind.

With Tends Hearth's hand in mine and Three Fingers at our side, our tiny colony heads north. Perhaps someday, our tiny homestead will grow to become a new village.

We are fortunate that winter is late this year. We hike for twelve days, and finally, at dusk, we reach the clearing where I convalesced after the mountain lion attack. Three Fingers asks if this is where we'll spend the winter. "No, we're not there yet." I notice Three Fingers and Tends Hearth make eye contact. I'm certain that my vision is of a place that remains farther north.

Nevertheless, I'm glad that we have found this clearing again. It is tempting to spend the winter here. There's already a shelter, and the almost-completed ground cache miraculously has protected a store of dried meat that we can make good use of. I'm glad to have the treasures we were forced to leave behind. I show Tends Hearth the egg-shaped rock and the mountain lion teeth and claws that Ferocious Wind had saved. I decide not to tell her that her sister had meant for the teeth and claws to be a wedding present. I'm glad to have my monk's robe, and more importantly, the spiral medallion. I notice that Tends Hearth frowns at the sight of the charm.

It is hard to leave the clearing. It feels like I am turning my back on Ferocious Wind. I have a sense that her wild spirit resides here. Before we leave, I take the skin of the mountain lion that she had staked out. I think of how Ferocious Wind killed the giant cat and saved my life. I wish I could have saved her life as well. It begins to snow as we set out, and Tends Hearth and Three Fingers try to convince me we should remain here. I know they're hungry, cold, and tired. Stubbornly I insist on continuing northward.

Several days later, we arrive in another clearing near a wide, rushing river at the foot of a large mountain that I believe is welcoming us. It's not Skellig Michael, of course, but it has a striking, powerful appearance of its own. I was sure I'd know the right spot when I saw it and I have no hesitation that this is the place I was meant to find. After a lifetime of bad luck, it's almost a miracle that nothing bad happened on our way. I'm relieved. I say a grateful prayer and ask God to continue to bless us.

I wander around the clearing, looking at it from each direction. I set my pack basket on the ground and sit on a rock, my hand on my chin. Three Fingers sits on the ground a few feet away, crosses his legs, straightens his back, tips his head back and closes his eyes, as if in prayer. Tends Hearth sits beside me on the rock. "Are we home now?"

I nod, turn toward her, and kiss her cheek. "Where would you like me to build our house?"

She turns her head right, left, then back toward me and suggests that we build our home around the rock that we're sitting on.

I imagine tapping on the rock during the winter. I think I can sculpt it into a comfortable seat. "Which direction should the doorway face?"

Tends Hearth suggests that the door face toward the river, south by southwest. "How are we going to build it before winter comes?" She asks what the house will look like and suggests that we build a quick wickiup for the winter, then perhaps a small longhouse next summer.

I shake my head and smile. I have an idea in my head. I don't know if it will work, but while we hiked the northbound trail, I recalled the day by the river when I moved stones through the power of concentration. What if I can do that here? I don't want to tell her my idea until I see if it will work. "Let me think about it for a couple of hours, then we'll get started."

Tends Hearth suggests that she can build a fire. I tell her she should build the fire where she wants it to be when our home is built. She begins gathering wood from the forest that surrounds the clearing. Three Fingers rises from his seat on the ground. He looks tired. I'm glad we have arrived so that he will not have to hike any longer. I suggest that he fish in the river. It's our best chance for a meal today. I walk with Three Fingers toward the river, turn, and tell Tends Hearth to holler if she needs me. I know she doesn't like to be left alone outdoors.

I help Three Fingers gather bait from the forest floor and get him settled comfortably by the river. Then I pace along the side of the river, arms crossed over my chest. The river is a perfect source for the rocks I will need to build a rock home, like the ones we built at Skellig Michael. The rocks aren't shaped the same, but I imagine I can get them to fit together.

A rock that looks too big to carry catches my eye. I focus an intent gaze on the rock and concentrate on the fact that I would like the rock to rise from the riverbed. I jump up and down in celebration. I lose my concentration and the rock tumbles back into the river with a giant splash.

I turn to look at Three Fingers, who has jumped to his feet and stands pointing at the spot in the river where the rock had risen, floated in the air, then tumbled back into the river. His other hand holds the wooden stick that is tied to his line. A commotion in the river forces his attention away from my levitation experiment.

My eyes return to the rocks in the river. One by one, I politely request a dozen boulders move from their watery home and I watch them float up the path toward our homestead. I can almost see our clearing from the river, but not quite. I will need to set the rocks down, then move myself to a place where I can move them again before placing them in our little meadow within the forest.

I can see Tends Hearth a short distance away, carrying a large branch toward the small fire she has built near the rock we sat on earlier. I look away from her and focus on the first rock. In my mind, I ask it to move.

I'm still amazed that such a thing is possible, and I am more astonished that it is something *I* can do. The rock lifts and hovers a foot above the ground, then moves toward our clearing. Wherever I look, that's where the rock goes.

When Tends Hearth sees the rock floating toward the clearing, she drops the branch and gapes at the sight. I can't help but smile, just a little, careful to maintain sufficient concentration on the rock. When it is safely resting on the ground, I turn my gaze to the next rock and move it to a spot beside the first.

With the first batch of rocks ready in the clearing, I run to Tends Hearth. I sweep her into my arms and kiss her lips. Then, with her still in my arms, I tilt my head back slightly, look into her eyes and ask, "How about if I build us a stone house instead of one made from wood?"

Two days later, I must have a thousand rocks in our little clearing. It looks like the debris field that is left behind after a flood or an avalanche. I feel like a king commanding an invisible army as I effortlessly move stones from one place to another. The biggest boulders secure the foundation. The higher I go, the smaller the rocks become. I wish that I could make the roof from rock as well. I'm not confident in my engineering and building skills, and I worry about the roof collapsing during a winter storm. Instead I cover our home with a wood and thatch roof, just as we did on my island back home. At the entrance, I pile rocks, creating a short tunnel that we cover with deer hides. Making a more permanent door is a big priority. We'll need that to feel safe. I hope to construct a sturdy door in the next couple of days.

Our stone home isn't nearly as big as a longhouse, but there is plenty of room for the three of us. The fire warms the stone that holds the heat and keeps us warm. The little chimney that I made draws the smoke upward and keeps it from choking us. I worried that I'd have to experiment with that.

We spend the next day plugging all of the holes that we can. Whenever possible, we place rocks and stones in the gaps. In the smallest holes, we push branches through until they're plugged. Our home is finished just in time to welcome our first blizzard. It snows for two days and we keep ourselves busy inside making snowshoes. We're going to need them.

Chapter 25

We are without food and I'm on the trail looking for game on one of the coldest days of winter. We're increasingly distressed about the emptiness of our cook pot. I enjoy being outside, but I'm disappointed that I have failed to find food this morning. I worry that I shouldn't have made the trip north so late in the season. I was warned not to.

I think about whether to return home and warm myself at the fire before heading out again. I'm standing in a clearing on a hillside with a nice view of the river. It is a short distance from our home. I'm overwhelmed by a strange and unfamiliar feeling. I don't know what compels me to step from the game path into the clearing. I feel a surge of energy, yet I feel dizzy at the same time.

I take another step and I walk through shimmering air. Abruptly, instead of a winter morning, it's a balmy autumn day. I'm standing in freshly fallen colorful leaves, and I feel as though I have been moved from one place to another. Only, it is the same exact place. How can it be fall instead of winter?

I wander up the path in the opposite direction of my stone house, though I don't know why. What compels me to walk in this direction? The path has quickly turned from a narrow game trail to a wide lane that only humans could have made. That turns into a thick flat surface that feels like stone beneath my feet, but looks too uniform to be natural stone. A pair of strange yellow lines divide the road beneath my feet.

A short distance down this path, I see a building. It is set a short distance from the stone road with the yellow lines. It's a handsome cabin. Its log walls look perfectly uniform. I wonder at the uniformity of the logs. There are no signs of the woodsman's axe on the surface of the logs. No two trees are the same and yet each log in the cabin appears identical. The door to the cabin stands open.

I step up to the door, peek around, and look for people. I don't see anyone anywhere. I tentatively step into the cabin. The furnishings remind me of the kinds of tables and chairs used by the monks at Skellig Michael, but this cabin has some strange items that I don't recall from the monastery.

There is but one room in this cabin, and a loft up some stairs overlooks the room. Everything in the cabin is tidy. Someone has cleaned it recently. Some sort of baked good sits on a ledge by an open window. I walk to the window and breathe in the delicious, fruity smell that reminds me of berries. I hold my hand above it and I can feel its heat. It's been so long since I've eaten. I reach for the dish and my hands pass through it, unable to grasp it. I'm surprised and I try again.

In this strange place, I am a spirit. That means I must be dead. Such a realization is hard to accept. I find the need to grieve my own passing, but that sentiment is short-lived. Perhaps that's the way it is when you are a spirit.

As I investigate further, I find a painting of a man and a woman on the wall. Only, in this painting, the subjects appear lifelike. I can't discern any brush strokes. The man has bright white teeth and thick blond hair that looks unnaturally neat and tidy. The woman has a strange pile of hair on her head, bright yellow and white clothing, and some strange contraption perched on her nose so that you can't see her eyes. I place my face even closer, and I can see the image of an older man. He appears to be wearing the robe of a monk. He has a thin, weathered face, and a long grey beard. He doesn't look the same as the man and the woman, and he looks strangely out of place. His image is opaque, like he has been drawn from fog. I feel like I'm looking at myself as an old man. Then I'm startled at the realization that it *is* me in the painting. How can it be? I wonder whether this man or this woman in the picture are somehow related to me, only in the future.

I see a small, box-shaped object sitting on a long table. It has numbers on it. As I'm looking at it, one of the numbers flips. Instead of 2:31, it now says 2:32. The plastic box is connected by some kind of thick string to the wall.

Next to the object with the flipping numbers, I see a yellow booklet. I bend to look at it closely. In big black letters, it says, "The Old Farmer's Almanac." A four digit number appears in the middle of the cover: 1984. At the top of the booklet it says, "192nd Anniversary Edition" and at the side where the book is bound it reads, "Published Every Year Since 1792." I do some quick figuring. If my numbers are correct, it is 1434 years in the future. It is no wonder that I'm a spirit.

I hear music in the distance. I follow the sound and find it coming from within another small box that is connected to the wall. A singing woman's voice repeatedly asks the question, "What's love got to do with it?" I marvel at the notion that music can come from a box. There's nobody in this cabin singing, and nobody is here listening either, and yet there *is* music.

Next to the music box is another strange-looking object. There's a small string of dots hanging from a shiny cylinder, under a conical covering of some sort. I concentrate on the shiny beads until the string is pulled. It snaps back into the cylinder and light floods the room. I jump in surprise. I've seen enough of such objects, and I rush back through the open door.

Outside, I wander around the cabin. I notice that the cabin is surrounded by very short grass that is uniformly sized, perhaps a couple of inches thick. There is more of this grass behind the cabin. Beyond that, I see trees at the edge of a forest.

A slight movement catches my attention. It appears that there is a man near one of the trees. He is wearing a red shirt with overlapping dark squares on it. His legs are blue; perhaps it is some kind of fabric that he's wearing on his legs. He also wears blue shoes on his feet. I wander closer to get a better look. He lowers himself to a sitting position beneath the maple tree, his arms resting on his knees and his head in his hands. He seems sad, or distressed.

I step a little closer. The man has a long length of rope in his lap. I see him make a loop at one end of it. Then he wraps one side of the rope around the other, fashioning the rope into a noose. I'm overwhelmed by sadness and angst. What could cause a young man like that to do such a thing? I wonder if stopping him is the reason that I'm here. But how can I stop him? How long do I have? What can I possibly do to prevent what I can plainly see is just about to happen?

I hear a knocking behind me. It startles me, and I can't find the source of the knocking. Whatever it is will have to wait. I turn back to look at the man under the tree. He is standing now, and he is tying a knot around a stone at the end of the rope, opposite the noose.

Then he throws the rock up and over a thick branch of the maple tree, eighteen feet above the ground. The rope follows the rock, and the rock lands on the ground a short distance away. The man unties the rock from the rope and pulls the rope behind him. There is a large boulder ten feet away. He ties the rope securely to the big rock and returns to the tree. I feel his sense of hopelessness as he looks up into the tree and sees the noose hanging. It would seem that the rope is the perfect length for what he has in mind.

I have a hunch that this man is related to the people in the painting on the cabin wall. Maybe he is their son. Somehow, I can't help but think that he is related to me as well.

It looks like he is drinking from some manner of container that is wrapped in a bark-colored sack. After a while, I see him toss the sack into the woods and it makes a clinking sound as the contents of the container break upon impact. The man doesn't flinch at the sound.

He climbs until he's sitting on the branch that the noose hangs from. Slowly he pulls the rope until he's holding the knot in his hands. I look back and forth quickly, trying to figure out what I can do. When I look back at the man, he's placing the noose over his head and pushing the knot against his neck. I run around the tree like a crazy man. Why am I here? What can I do?

I look up and see that the man is rising to his feet. This is it. He is preparing to jump. His legs bend, and I'm sure that he is about to leap from the branch.

In a fraction of an instant, I remember that I can enter the tree. I consider it a miracle that somehow this healthy tree drops its living limb. I hear it crash to the ground as my spirit separates from the tree.

A hundredth of a second later, I levitate the big rock with my open palms toward the sky. It turns out that it isn't necessary.

He has landed heavily on the ground. His breath has been knocked from his lungs, and he gasps for air like he has a will to live. I can see that he is scraped up, but he appears to be unharmed. I move the boulder so that it is directly above his head.

He looks up at the rock that hangs over him, and he shields his head with his arm. Then he rolls away so that the rock no longer hovers above him.

I lower the rock slowly and I see the look of astonishment on his face. From where I stand, he no longer looks like a man. Perhaps he's in his late teens. With one upward-facing palm, I maintain the rock directly in front of him. With my other arm, I direct small stones to levitate from beneath the leaves on the forest floor. They gather, swirling around us under the maple tree. Their movement reminds me of the slow swirl of Tends Hearth's spoon in her cook pot. The young man's mouth hangs open and his body shivers in fear.

It strikes me that I should speak to him. What can I say? I set the boulder on the ground and gather the flying stones into a pile as he watches. I approach him so that I'm inches in front of his face. I cite Lector Beccán's favorite prayer. The man turns his head slightly, innocently, like he's listening to a distant voice that he can't quite hear. It doesn't matter. He doesn't need to hear the prayer for it to have power.

I place my hand on his shoulder. He shrinks from my touch at first, then his face fills with an expression that I would describe as wonder, or maybe it is hopefulness. Touching his shoulder isn't like touching the plate of food by the window in the cabin. It is more like the sensation that I got when I passed through the shimmering air. I place my other hand on his opposite shoulder. His eyes widen further. He crosses his arms over his chest, placing his hands on top of mine. Then I kiss him, on one cheek and then the other. I withdraw my hands from his shoulders and step back.

The man touches his cheeks gently with the tips of his fingers, then he looks at the tips of his fingers. I hear him say, "I've been kissed by God. God loves me. Oh, how can it be?" Then he cries into his hands, asking, "Oh, what have I done?"

I place my hand on his shoulder. I tell him not to worry about the past, and then I tell him to share God's love with the world. He nods like he understands me. I back away from him, and I can see his gaze follow my departure. I turn my back to him and return along the path that led me here. I laugh at the thought that this young man thinks that he encountered God. It was only me in front of him, not God, but without God, such moments would never be possible.

As an afterthought, I turn back toward the man. I raise my palms and summon the boulder. I set the big rock on the ground just outside the door of the cabin. Then I call the stones and pile them on the other side of the cabin door. I'm taking a chance that the young man lives in this cabin. I want to give him something to remember, something that he can wonder about, and something that he will never forget.

I hope that I did what I was supposed to do. I think of my little family—my wife and the healer. I hope that I'm able to find my way back to them. I'm supposed to be hunting so that we can eat.

When I return to the magical spot on the hill overlooking the river, I'm grateful to find that the air still shimmers. What's love got to do with it? Everything, I suppose.

As I pass through the shimmering air, I return from autumn in the distant future to the cold winter day of the present. As I hurry home, I wonder: am I able to break the curse? Is that poor man by the tree suffering from the wretched curse that was placed upon me? What can I do to end such misery? How will I ever know?

Chapter 26

Tends Hearth sleeps at my side and it is well after dark. I should be asleep. I can't stop thinking of the man at the maple tree and the strange cabin in the woods. I recall the smell of warm baked goods and the memory makes my hunger more desperate. We consumed the last of our food the day before yesterday. If we don't find food soon, our situation will become dire. There's nothing I can do about it now, except to be prepared to hunt, first thing in the morning.

My thoughts turn to stone, as they often do. Now that we have a protective stone house to keep us safe and warm through the winter, I fantasize about what else I would like to create. I hold my hand over the spiral medallion that hangs from a cord on my chest. I close my eyes and imagine the spiral depicted in stepping stones in a giant circle on the ground. As my finger traces the endless line on the face of the medallion, I visualize myself walking from stone to stone. I imagine walking the pattern, into the center and then back out again, never stepping on the same rock twice. I feel a sense of strength, knowledge, and love. I resolve to begin constructing this earthwork as soon as spring comes, if we survive the winter. My need for sleep overcomes my need for food.

In the morning, I feel an intense vibration. It feels like the whole world is shaking. I open my eyes. It's dark and blurry. I worry that the vibrations will cause our stone home to cave in on us. Then I feel my foot shake violently, as if someone has grabbed it. I sit up and rub my eyes. I can make out the sleeping forms of Tends Hearth by my side and Three Fingers across the fire. I sit, stunned, not knowing what to do or think.

Again, I have the sensation that my foot has been grabbed, and I can see my foot moving, as if being shaken by an unseen hand. Fear of the unknown has me frozen, unable to move. I wonder if this is how the man by the tree felt when he encountered me.

As I'm looking at the entrance to our home, I see my bow that was leaning against the wall fall to the ground, as if blown over by a swift breeze. Then my quiver of arrows tumbles over as well. As I try to contrive a logical explanation for how that could have happened, I feel a familiar grip on my ankle, and my foot shakes once more. I feel a breeze across my arm and a thought crosses my mind. It is time to hunt. I dress fast, grab my fallen bow, my quiver of arrows, and optimistically lift an empty pack basket over my shoulders.

I feel a tug at my chest, similar to the tug I often feel at the center of my stomach. I don't know where I'm headed. Maybe it is instinct that I'm following, only I feel like I'm being led somewhere. I realize that the place I'm drawn to is the spot where yesterday, the air shimmered, and I found myself transformed.

I wonder whether that place is somewhere I should avoid, or whether I am destined to return there frequently. As I round the final bend in the trail, I see that magical place. The air shimmers, visibly. Prior to yesterday, the only time I can remember having seen the air shake is on the hottest of summer days, when the blazing heat seems to appear above the surface of a heated rock.

As I turn the bend in the trail, I see that magical place. Standing in the spot where I stood is a massive buck, and he is the biggest stag I've ever seen. His head turns slightly in my direction. It seems to me that he is looking into my eyes. He tips his head toward me, and I wonder how he can balance such a massive structure on top of his head. I feel hunger gnawing at my gut, and I wonder whether the tip of his head is significant. Then he turns his body as if he's inviting me to launch an arrow between his ribs. My arrow flies fast and true, and drops the biggest deer I have ever seen. He makes no attempt to flee. My aim isn't always so good, though it was close range. I can't help but think that my arrow was guided by the unseen hand that shook my foot.

Usually, I approach a dead or dying animal cautiously. Instead, I rush to the side of the downed deer like I'm hurrying to the side of a fallen comrade. I toss my bow aside and drop to the ground. I throw my arms around the animal. I bury my face in his thick winter coat and thank him for his sacrifice. His body is warm. I stroke his fur and say a prayer. Today, I shall be able to feed my wife and our friend.

I feel the air shimmer above me again, as it did yesterday, and I am reminded of the power of this unusual place. My fingers grab greedily at the body of the deer. I'm afraid that the deer will disappear, leaving us to starve. I must prevent that if I can. I stand and gather his hoofs together, hoping to drag him from the spot where he fell. Unfortunately, he is too heavy, and I can't get him to move.

I reach for my knife. I shall have to butcher him in place. We shall not waste the gift we have received. Every part of this deer will be gratefully put to good use. As I sink my knife into the stag's flesh, it occurs to me that I was led to the deer by Ferocious Wind. But how could that be? She is dead. Then I think about how, just yesterday, I appeared as a spirit and helped a man in need. I remind myself of the miracles that God performs. My mouth waters, and I think of the meal that we'll have cooking over our fire. No more thoughts of miracles—I must focus on harvesting every bit of this magnificent specimen.

I am covered in blood and I must look a fright as I return home with a heavy pack. Tends Hearth rushes to help me unload the abundance of meat while Three Fingers gets his pack basket. I can smell the first cut of venison on our fire as I rush from our home. I wonder how many trips it will take to bring the big deer home. My mouth waters and I consider taking a big bite of raw meat, but there's no time for that. We must bring everything back before competing carnivores attempt to share in our bounty.

Fortunately, it is a short distance from our home to the carcass. I haven't been gone long, hardly long enough to unload my pack basket and return. This time when I round the bend I see a big brown wolverine perched on top of the buck, teeth bared, claws extended, nose turned up defensively. Fortunately, I have my bow and arrows with me. Sometimes I forget to carry them, and I always admonish myself when I do. Unlike my homeland, I must always be ready for danger at every step here.

Normally, wolverines hunt at night. This one must have a den nearby. The smell of our kill must have brought it out despite the daylight.

I notch an arrow and send it flying. It appears to graze the back of the wily wolverine which needs no more convincing. Even so, I keep a cautious eye out as I reclaim my kill, remembering the raccoon that ripped the face from Tends Hearth's baby sister.

In our home, Tends Hearth has venison drying all around the fire. The deer's antlers are draped with strips of drying meat. Hastily constructed drying racks hold slowly cooking meat. I wish we could stop and eat our fill, but we have one more trip to make. We set our pack baskets down and race back to the carcass. We drag what remains by the hooves.

I work with Tends Hearth to process the meat. Three Fingers grinds the brains of the deer. He will use the paste to cure the hide. If we're thrifty, this one big kill could carry us through the winter.

After days of working on the carcass it's nice to sit and do nothing for a few minutes. I should be crafting things we need for our survival rather than lolling by the fire, watching my wife stir the pot. At least several times a day, I remind myself that I have a wife. I don't know why I find it so shocking, but a year ago, I would never have thought such a thing possible.

As I watch Tends Hearth cook, I marvel at the magnificence of her back. What she thinks of as a deformity, I find beautiful. When we embrace, I love to glide my hand across the skin on her back and visualize the symbol.

In the dim firelight of our stone abode, I blink in surprise at the sight of it. Its color has transformed from red to luminescent amber. My heart races in excitement. I jump to my feet and embrace her from behind, wrapping my hands around her belly. My chest is pressed against her back. I close my eyes and I can feel myself transported, my spirit flowing through her bloodstream, just as I traveled through the trunks of trees. Each beat of her heart pulls me in one direction, then pumps me in another. One particular heartbeat sends me through a narrow tube that connects her to a miniature human, one so small that it is hard to fathom it becoming big enough to be a child, let alone an adult. My own heart feels as if it might burst at the realization that my wife is carrying a child. I wonder if she knows. I open my eyes and my spirit returns to my body. I turn her toward me and she drops her wooden spoon into the cook pot. As I pull her toward our sleeping mat, I see Three Fingers reach for his fishing stick.

Our lovemaking is slow and tender, less urgent than when we were first married. Now that we have a home and have secured sustenance, it doesn't seem as frivolous to laze about enjoying the aftermath of our coupling.

After we have been intimate, I feel an elevated sense of exultation. With my wife's head resting on my chest, I am calm, happy, and relaxed, and I feel like anything is possible. I feel invincible and immortal, until Tends Hearth whispers that she wishes that she were her sister instead of herself. I reassure my wife that I am glad she is not. I tell her that she is perfect as she is, and I wouldn't want for her to be anyone else. She tells me that she is sure I must have loved Ferocious Wind because she was wild and exciting. She asks me whether I found it more pleasurable to join with Ferocious Wind. I don't think she believes me when I tell her that we never did. I confess that I did love her sister, but reassure her that I now know that it was always her that I was meant to marry. She seems to accept what I'm telling her when I tell her that I'm happier than I could ever imagine being.

Tends Hearth has come to accept that I can lift objects with my thoughts. After a couple of weeks, even the most unbelievable things can seem ordinary. I haven't told her about how my spirit can jump from my body and the strange journeys it can make. For starters, I tell her that I think that a child grows within her. She's shocked at the news, but doesn't think to ask how I could know such a thing. "You'll see," I tell her.

We spend a few minutes laughing and dreaming about the possibilities of what our children might look like, or what they might accomplish. Will our family become a village someday?

Three Fingers returns from the river. It's too cold for an old man to spend too much time alone outdoors this time of year. Tends Hearth rises from our mats to retrieve the wooden spoon from her pot. She scoops a hearty portion of stew into a bowl and hands it to me while Three Fingers cleans the small fish that he extracted from the icy river.

I think of the man in the tree with the noose around his neck. I reflect on Spits Teeth and Bobcat Mask, and I hope that our children will not have to live in such a troubled world. My heart leaps at the thought and hope that perhaps they will make the world a better place. If only I could be sure that we are no longer cursed.

Chapter 27

Through the winter, I enjoy my life as a new husband and I think about impending fatherhood. I wonder how long it will take. Tends Hearth grows larger and larger. Three Fingers tells me that we still have several moon cycles to wait.

When I am not thinking about my family, I think about the stone spiral that I'm determined to construct. We've gathered plenty of provisions for our survival. The river holds a bounty of fish. There's no reason to delay any longer.

I wish that I had my mallet and the chisels, the ones I used to make the steps at Skellig Michael. I can make a new mallet, but I don't know how to find iron ore or smelt it. I've thought about it and I can't figure it out. I can chip away at one rock with another, but that makes for slow work. Still, that's exactly what I plan to do with the rock by the fire in our home. For the labyrinth, I shall search for similarly sized rocks with relatively flat surfaces.

I've selected a large, flat area near the banks of the river—it looks like the ideal site. I brush away leaves and smooth minor imperfections in the dirt. With a sharp stick, I painstakingly trace imaginary rocks depicting a spiral within a spiral. The design covers a large area, and I have left space between the stones, knowing that I will need to have extra room since I will not have the luxury of working with uniform shapes. I will probably have to settle for round and oval rocks. I'd rather have rocks that are shaped like bricks, but I shall make do with the rocks I find in the river.

Between fishing and gathering rocks for the labyrinth, I seem to spend most of my time by the river. Occasionally, I find good rocks in the forest when I'm gathering wood for our fire. After a hundred days, I have collected all the rocks that I will need, and I've set them on the ground. The next step is to bury them in the ground so that only the flat surface is exposed.

Still, Tends Hearth is getting bigger. I would have thought that the baby would have come by now. Three Fingers tells me to be patient. It is not yet time. Tends Hearth tries not to complain, but I can tell that she is not comfortable.

I hunch over and dig as fast as I can, laying stone after stone at the spiral. I wonder why I'm in such a hurry to complete this project. Sometimes I'm driven to do things, yet I'm at a loss to fully explain why. I'm excited to see it completed.

Finally, on a blazing hot day in the middle of summer, I'm sweating over what I know is the last stone in the design. I run toward the river, leaping into the air as I go.

I celebrate by bathing in the river. Tends Hearth is sitting on a rock with her feet in the river. She says that it relaxes her and keeps the swelling in her ankles to a minimum.

I tell her that I have completed the design and I ask if I can show it to her. She compliments the beauty of the design, then asks what it is for. I see her frown.

I tell her that the design is sacred. Walking the stone path and saying prayers brings the Great Spirit closer to us. He will know your heart and you will be closer to Him. Then I look at Tends Hearth and tell her that it is also supposed to be a fertility symbol. Walking the path might even help bring the baby. I tell her, "I shall walk the path as often as I can, and pray to God to lift the curse upon me."

It isn't easy to keep her feet on the path, but I manage to guide her, along one spiral to the center. We say a prayer together, then we follow the outbound spiral. She's tired when she finishes, and I help her get home. When she's comfortable on our sleeping mats, she asks me to lie down beside her.

She tells me that the spiral symbol reminds her of Ferocious Wind. She confesses that she is jealous of her sister and the image of the spiral always makes her feel stabs of jealousy. The spiral medallion I wear around my neck is especially hard for her to look upon. She's certain that the spiral pattern by the river is a monument to her sister.

I tell Tends Hearth that I would choose her if I had the chance to choose between her and Ferocious Wind. I ask her if it would make her feel better if I told her so every day. She nods. I should only have to tell her once, but if she takes comfort from it, I shall make it a habit. I conclude our conversation by saying that we should honor the memory of her sister and what she meant to us. It doesn't mean that I love her less because I also love her departed sister.

The sun sets late in the summertime. Three Fingers and Tends Hearth fall asleep swiftly, but I lie awake thinking about the curse. Making sure the curse is broken has become an obsession. I rise from our sleeping mat and walk through the dark starry night to the labyrinth.

I walk the path slowly, seeking comfort, solace, and grace. It is a dark night, with occasional wisps of fog, mostly rising from the surface of the river, tossed by a light breeze. After a particularly thick breeze, I see a woman standing in the center of the labyrinth.

I blink in surprise. I feel a pang of guilt. Tends Hearth is right, I shouldn't have made the labyrinth in the shape of a spiral. At the same time, I'm glad to see an image of Ferocious Wind. As I look upon her, I wonder if the man in the red shirt saw me as I see her.

It surprises me that she looks so calm and content. I flinch when she speaks to me. Seeing her reminds me of the day that her sister was hit by lightning, and how we found her company unbearable as we paddled the canoe. Her face seems serene. The wild look in her eyes is gone and she floats at ease, just above the ground rather than standing, ready to pounce. She seems much more at ease as a spirit than she did as a living being. Ferocious Wind confesses that she and her sister never were kindred spirits, but she loves her sister despite their differences.

Ferocious Wind tells me that she is glad that I have married Tends Hearth. She thinks that I am the only one who can understand the depth of loss she has experienced, having lost so many relatives. She also mentions the lasting impacts from the lightning strike. Ferocious Wind tells me to remember that Tends Hearth will forever carry that trauma with her.

Finally, Ferocious Wind says, "Everything that has happened *should* have happened. I was meant to love you, but we were not meant to be together. I was destined to be a warrior and to die as I lived. You were meant to learn the ways of war, and I was meant to teach you, but you were never meant to remain a warrior. I have come to know that we choose the lives we will live, before we are born. We enter the path, fully aware, but quickly forget. We gain strength and wisdom from our journey, and we exit the path wiser. Do not doubt yourself. Live, love, pray, and walk these steps as often as you can, for you were meant to do so. If you tell my sister that you saw me, tell her that I shall watch over you both."

I nod contentedly. It looks like she is tossing me a kiss on the back of her hand. Then, a light breeze comes along and sweeps her away.

I stand for a moment, trying to make sense of what just happened. It was not a conversation that we had. I don't think I spoke a word while I was in the presence of her spirit. Maybe she doesn't need to hear what I think about anything because she already knows.

Every word she said touched my soul as if she were telling me the things I needed to hear and know.

I step to the next stone, bow my head, and thank God for granting me another moment with Ferocious Wind.

Five years later, I'm sitting in the stone chair that I have carved from what I like to call *first rock*. It has been draped with the skin of the mountain lion and overlaid with other soft furs and hides.

Tends Hearth stands at the fire, stirring the contents of a clay cook pot. She seems happy and content. Our three small children play at her feet. Rowsheen is 4-years-old, Loegaire is one year younger, and Mochan is two years younger. Our daughter, Rowsheen takes after me. She has green eyes with brown specks in them, and straight, chestnut-colored hair. The boys take after their mother, with dark brown eyes and straight black hair. Tends Hearth insisted that I give them the kind of names they would have had if we lived where I was born. I can't remember meeting other children or hearing anything about them, so I named our sons after two of the monks, and our daughter is named for the mother I never met. I remember the day that our daughter was born. It was the last time I had the red and pink dream with the tug rope. I saw a vision of my mother, and I heard her name whispered in the breeze. My whole life, I have wished that I could know what my mother looked like. I wonder whether our daughter will grow up to resemble her grandmother.

Each season, Three Fingers appears thinner, weaker, and sicker, but he appears content nevertheless. He misses his partner and he mentions Gathers Seeds often, telling me about the plants he liked to collect, what they were used for, and how to prepare them. Three Fingers tells us that the spirits are calling him, but he isn't quite ready. Often he'll sit for hours wrapped in a comfortable robe, watching the children play. The look on his face reminds me of the look on Lector Beccán's face when he prayed. Last night, Three Fingers told me that he believes we have traveled the life path together several times. "I have been your father many times in the past, and I'm happy to have walked the world with you again in this lifetime." It troubled me to hear Three Fingers speak in the past tense, but I nodded anyhow. Recently, I've come to think of him more as a grandfatherly figure.

I should get up and head out into the day instead of lolling away the morning in the comfort of my chair. Despite the ability to levitate heavy objects, there is still much work to do to feed a hungry, growing family. I feel a tingly sensation along my shins as I rise. It's late, and Three Fingers still hasn't risen from his bunk. I place my hand on his shoulder to wake him, and I can tell that he has passed. His body is still warm, but he is not breathing and I cannot feel his pulse. I roll him onto his back, straighten his limbs, and cover him with his favorite deerskin blanket.

I speak quietly to Tends Hearth before stepping out of our home. I walk a short distance to the clearing where the air sometimes shimmers, the place where I was transported into the future. I beckon three enormous rocks, so large that an entire village couldn't move them with their collective strength. I set two rocks near each other, with twelve feet of clearance between them. The third rock is a long, thick slab. I place that rock on the ground in front of the other two rocks. I stand and admire the structure that frames the spot where strange things happen. I can't wait to place the long slab on top of it. Then I return home to retrieve the healer's body. When I get there, his body is gone.

I look at Tends Hearth. She can see the shock and horror on my face. I ask, "What happened?"

She looks about our home, as if she expects to see him. It's not that big a space. He could not have left our house without her knowing that he had gone.

I tell her that I want to show her something. She doesn't like leaving our home and the clearing that surrounds it, and never ventures into the woods without me at her side. I lift Loegaire onto my hip, and Tends Hearth picks up Mochan. Rowsheen follows us cheerfully.

A couple of minutes later, we arrive in the small clearing and find Three Fingers's body lying on the long stone slab, perfectly wrapped and tied in his blankets. Tends Hearth looks into my face. I'm wondering how many miracles an ordinary man such as myself has a right to expect.

I lower my gaze to the slab on the ground. I extend my arms forward, hands facing upward and lift my hands toward the heavens, as if I were lifting the slab with my own hands. I set the long slab so that it rests with one end on each of the two massive boulders I had set previously.

This combination of rocks forms a space that feels strange to stand in. My head aches and my skin tingles. I feel like there is a strong spiritual power here. It is a gathering force, a force not fully realized. I don't know whether I revere the power that grows here, or fear it.

I pray to God to watch over the spirit of Three Fingers, only I realize that instead of naming the God of my childhood, I have prayed to the Great Spirit.

Epilogue

I can see an old woman and I can hear her voice. I know her story as though I have heard her tell it hundreds of times. She isn't just old, she is ancient, decades older than Hole in the Roof. This ancient woman sits by a fire and her family is gathered around her, listening intently. The stars twinkle brightly against the dark blue sky and the light of a full moon casts a warm glow. A thin old man asks her to tell the creation story. A young boy, perhaps his grandson, sits by his side, eager to hear it.

She sits against a supportive rack. A thick bearskin softens her support structure, and another is wrapped around her, warming and concealing her body. I see her wince in pain as she settles her back against the rack. The simplest of movements can be painful for extremely aged people.

The woman begins, "Usually we tell children that the first person came from a giant turtle in the sky." Her gaze is locked directly on the child and she ignores the presence of the others who are also listening.

Stoically, she continues. "In fact, it was a giant, floating island in the sky. It *was* shaped like a turtle. The shell was made out of a smooth, shiny, golden brown, rock-like substance. It was very strong. It was as big as our mountain. It floated in the sky above the earth. All over the island there were bright, blinking lights, as numerous as

the stars in the sky, except that the lights were all different colors."
She stops to rest for a moment. Even quiet, her presence commands attention. I can just barely make out her dark eyes among the excess skin beneath her eyebrows. The dark maze of wrinkles on her cheeks and neck remind me of the bark of an old tree.

"At that time there was no land, just water everywhere. The people in the flying turtle wanted there to be land, in addition to the water."

She paused again, then whispered in a raspy voice, "Usually, we tell children that Sky Woman fell to earth from a hole in the flying turtle accompanied by the tallest tree that ever existed. We call that tree the Tree of Life. We also tell children that birds caught her and gently lowered her to the surface of the water. She asked the animals to help create the land by scooping dirt from the depths of the water and spreading dirt on the back of a big turtle. Then the dirt expanded until all the land had been created."

She is silent. Half a minute goes by. It seems as if she wants everyone to picture what she is saying. Just when I begin to think that she has lost her place in the story, she continues in a thunderous voice. I wouldn't have thought that she could speak so loudly. "What *really* happened is that the people in the flying turtle made the land rise from beneath the water by shooting massive light beams from the bottom of their flying boat, light beams millions of times more powerful than the light from the moon. Bubbling, fiery red and black dirt shot up into the sky. Time hung agelessly for the people in the boat in the sky. Beneath them, the ground took many years to form. The earth shook, and mountains spit forth from beneath the water."

She takes a couple of deep breaths and clears her throat. "A celestial named Sky Woman rode in a smaller floating boat which came out of the giant, flying turtle in the sky. It lowered her to the earth. She brought lots of things with her, in little containers that looked like they were made of frozen ice, only they were not cold, and they did not melt. She opened some of the containers and blew dust into the wind. Seeds."

A middle-aged man hands the ancient grandmother a wooden cup of cool water. She wets her lips, swooshes the water around within her cheeks, then swallows and continues. "Sky Woman was pregnant, and soon she had a daughter. When her daughter was old enough to have children of her own, Sky Woman used the contents of the magic containers on her ship to create life within her daughter. Sky Woman's daughter had twin boys. She named them Sapling and Flint. Eventually there were enough descendants of Sky Woman that she no longer needed the contents of the magic vessels to bring forth life."

She rests briefly before resuming. "This is the secret story. It is the story told at Women's Council meetings. This is the story known to the seers of our people. Sky Woman is our great-grandmother, ten thousand generations in the past." She pauses before concluding. "We are descended from her. The Great Spirit sent her to create our people on this earth."

The young boy by the fire tentatively asks, "Where is Sky Woman's ship now?"

"I don't know, but I would like to see it too."

"What did Sky Woman look like?"

"I don't know, but she is a part of all of us. I expect she looked a lot like we do," the woman concludes.

The boy asks about the first men, Sapling and Flint. She tells him about their trouble getting along. "One was good. One was evil. Fortunately, good won out over evil as it does eventually because the Great Spirit is wise and benevolent. Though many times we do not understand the Great Spirit."

The boy asks, "Where did the rest of the people on the flying turtle go?"

"I don't know, but I've thought a lot about it. I think they were placed several different places on this earth, and then I think the flying turtle traveled on to other, far away places, dropping people wherever they could find a suitable home for them. Just look out into the sky at night. There must be lots of places where children are asking the same questions you are asking tonight."

My family listens as I tell them this story. Rowsheen opens her mouth to ask a question.

I reach forward and place my hand on her ankle. "How do I know about the essence of trees, the powerful web of energy that reverberates from stone, and the cosmic tug that pulls us along? I don't. It could all be just a dream. What I do know is that there is a God, whether God manifests as a tree or appears in the form of a wise old matriarch, or in some other manner. There is a higher power. Life is cyclical. It has meaning. We continue beyond the death of our vessels. Very few people are fortunate to be able to hear the voice of God. I have heard that voice and that is how I know that *I* was once Sky Woman, I am not just descended from her. Now you know me as your father, Conchobar. The old woman who will tell the creation story to her great-grandson will not be born for hundreds of years. Don't ask me how I know that; I just do."

I close my eyes and experience a vision in which time speeds by. I see a collection of future moments, and I'm taken from one brief scene to another.

In the first one, perhaps it is a year or two from now, as Rowsheen appears just a little taller and older. She enters the labyrinth and playfully hops from rock to rock. I follow her solemnly. After a couple of steps she stops and looks toward the center of the labyrinth. I ask Rowsheen if she knows who that woman is. She nods bravely, and it occurs to me that Rowsheen has seen her before. The ghost of Ferocious Wind proclaims, "I am Rowsheen's angel." Rowsheen nods vigorously, accepting it as fact. I think that she has heard it before. I feel an ache in my chest as it seems that Rowsheen is growing up way too quickly.

In the next scene, I see adults that look like they could be my children. There is a stone building set into the hillside at the edge of the clearing where we have built our home. Inside that cave-like structure is an inner tomb. I see these people carrying my body into the tomb. Then they conceal the tomb within the stone building. Finally they cover the stone structure with dirt. It almost looks as if the hillside is untouched by human hands.

Inside the dark tomb, time speeds quickly and I see my body turn to bones. I get the sense that hundreds of years are floating by in a matter of seconds. Then there is light. Someone has discovered the cave. It is the man I saw at the fire with the ancient grandmother and his grandson, the boy she spoke to. He is there too, only he is older.

More time passes, perhaps hundreds of years. I see dust growing thick on my skeletal remains. My bones have gone dry with the passage of time. Someone has found the hidden chamber. I see someone's silhouette, peering into the tomb.

Who has discovered my bones? My vision becomes clearer. It is the man who tried to hang himself. The man who believed that he was kissed by God.

My Humble Request

As a new indie author, I'm striving to help my books find an audience. Nothing is more valuable in helping people find my books than reviews from readers like you. Even a very short review is enormously helpful, and I will be most grateful. Thank you so much for your interest in my book.

Also by David Fitz-Gerald

From The Adirondack Spirit Series

Wanders Far—An Unlikely Hero's Journey
Wanders Far lived in dangerous times and was faced with one difficult challenge after another. From a very young age, his wanderlust compelled him down one path after another. He was happy living a simple life in the physical world. The spirit world had other plans. One lifetime was not enough for Wanders Far's old soul.

https://books2read.com/wandersfar

*She Sees Ghosts—The Story of a Woman Who Rescues Lost Soul*s
As a young girl, Mehitable had ignored the apparitions that she never spoke of. Ghosts of the Revolutionary War needed help that only she could provide. Would she save the spirits' souls or would they save her? Fans of TV's *Ghost Whisperer* and *Long Island Medium* will especially love *She Sees Ghosts.*

https://books2read.com/sheseesghosts

Information about future installments in the series can be found at https://www.itsoag.com/

Not part of the Adirondack Spirit Series

In the Shadow of a Giant—Remembering Paleface Ski Center and Dude Ranch

The story of a dreamer who fought Mother Nature, Father Time, and a dwindling checkbook balance to build a family-owned resort in the heart of the Adirondack Mountains. Take a trip back in time and enjoy a one-of-a-kind, vintage, Adirondack vacation experience.

https://books2read.com/itsoag

Thank you for reading *The Curse of Conchobar.*

CPSIA information can be obtained
at www.ICGtesting.com
Printed in the USA
FSHW011109290421
80817FS

9 781977 238153